THE CADEN CHRONICLES

DEAD MAN'S HAND

ZONDERKIDZ

A portion of the profits from the sale of *Dead Man's Hand* will go to Heart of the Horse Therapy Ranch, committed to promoting therapeutic riding by developing community awareness of equine assisted / facilitated therapy. HHTR serves the physically challenged and those suffering from emotional or behavioral disorders.

Nick and the rest of the Caden family invite you to saddle up and help. To learn more visit: http://heartofthehorseranch.com or email: heartofthehorsetherapy@gmail.com

Dead Man's Hand
Copyright © 2012 by Eddie Jones

This title is also available as a Zondervan ebook.
Visit www.zondervan.com/ebooks

Requests for information should be addressed to:
Zonderkidz, 5300 Patterson Ave. SE, Grand Rapids, Michigan 49530

Library of Congress Cataloging-in-Publication Data

Jones, Eddie, 1957-
    Dead man's hand / by Eddie Jones.
        p. cm. — (The Caden chronicles; bk. 1)
    Summary: When fourteen-year-old Nick Caden vacations at Deadwood Canyon Ghost Town, he finds himself in the middle of a mystery involving ghosts of infamous dead outlaws, disappearing dead bodies, and murders.
        ISBN 978-0-310-72344-8
        [1. Ghost towns—Fiction. 2. Ghosts—Fiction. 3. Robbers and outlaws—Fiction. 4. Mystery and detective stories.] I. Title.
PZ7.J68534De 2012
[Fic]—dc23   2012027549

Published in association with Heartline Literary Agency, Pittsburg, PA, 15235.

Zonderkidz is a trademark of Zondervan.

Cover design: Sammy Yuen
Editor: Kim Childress
Illustrations: Owen Richardson
Interior design: Sarah Molegraaf

Printed in the United States of America

12 13 14 15 16 17 /DCI/ 24 23 22 21 20 19 18 17 16 15 14 13 12 11 10 9 8 7 6 5 4 3 2 1

DEDICATED TO my son Win who encouraged me to swing for the fence. Thanks, buddy. Your word of encouragement on our sail to Beaufort all those years ago means more than you'll ever know.

SPECIAL THANKS TO ... Bennie Jones ... who allows me to write and pursue my heart's desire. Cindy Sproles ... who constantly waves her pom poms and cheers me on. Diana Flegal ... who believes in this story, my writing, and my passion for young readers. JC, the original Dead Man ... whose hand continues to reach out in love to save us.

THE CADEN CHRONICLES

DEAD MAN'S HAND

BOOK ONE

EDDIE JONES

ZONDERVAN.com/
AUTHORTRACKER
follow your favorite authors

CHAPTER ONE
DEAD ON ARRIVAL

"**S**houldn't be long now," Dad said, tapping the windshield. "Just on the other side of those mountains." Through the front glass I saw a white sign that read: WELCOME TO DEADWOOD: GHOST TOWN IN THE SKY.

I slumped in my seat, the vehicle's rear window reflecting my wild tangle of unruly bangs and bored expression. Beyond the curves ahead lay the ragged spine of the Rockies and green glades of spruce and fir. Dad stomped the accelerator, causing the underpowered engine to whine as we rocketed up the two-lane blacktop toward Deadwood Canyon, where for five fun-filled days we would pan for gold in mountain streams (*Pan rentals extra*), stalk buffalo herds with Native American guides

(*Please, do not call your guide an "Indian"*), and learn to shoot and ride with Billy the Kid, Jesse James, and the Dalton Gang.

We cleared the mountain pass and banked around a curve. In the valley below stood a two-story hotel with a red roof and wraparound porch. Next to it a saloon, tannery shop, horse stables, and ... *what's that*? A bookstore offering a cowboy poetry reading? My younger sister the writer would be so thrilled. For weeks she'd talked of nothing except how much fun we would have on our summer vacation in the not-so-wild west. All I'd thought of was how I wished I could have gone to the video gaming convention in Vegas instead.

Mom touched the display on the GPS. "See, Frank? We're only two hours late."

"Wouldn't have been late at all if I hadn't followed that stupid contraption."

"*You* are the one who got us lost."

"Is it my fault the interstate was closed?"

"You could have followed the detour signs like everyone else."

"Yeah, and remained behind those eighteen-wheelers for who knows how long. My way was quicker."

"Sure, Frank. Whatever you say."

For most of the trip I'd managed to block out my parents bickering with a pair of form-fitted Skullcandy headphones, but a few miles outside of Golden, Colorado, the battery died on my iPod. Now Mom and Dad were at it again, ripping into each other and setting the tone for our "one big happy family" vacation. Bored, I stared into the valley at the large, furry bovine grazing on pastureland.

"Are those real buffalo?" my sister asked.

"Bison," I replied. "Buffalo are only found in Asia and Africa. Bison used to roam from the Great Bear Lake in Canada's far northwest to the western boundary of the Appalachian Mountains."

She replied, "Look like buffalo to me."

We reached the western side of the mountain range and entered the wide valley. A couple hundred yards past a road marker pointing toward a national park, Dad turned onto a gravel drive and parked our "toaster" car under a wooden archway decorated with cow horns and horseshoes. A sign announced: THIS WAY TO GUEST REGISTRATION AND LAZY JACK'S LIVERY STABLE. He pulled up to the guardhouse and rolled down his window. He waited a full five seconds before laying on the horn.

"For crying out loud, Frank. Chill!" Sighing, Mom fanned a hand through her cropped hair (bleached blonde to hide the gray) and fixed her pale gray eyes on Dad, who was drumming the steering wheel.

"Just letting them know we're here."

Dad popped the horn again. Two short beeps followed by a long blast.

"Really! You're so impatient."

Wendy rolled down her window and pointed. "Look at those cabins. They're just like I pictured in *Comanche and the Cowboy*. I hope we get one that backs up to the creek."

"I'm sure wherever we stay will be fine," Mom said.

Bet not. Bet we have to use an outhouse and bathe in a creek. They probably don't even have cell coverage in this hole. I reached into my pocket and checked. Sure enough, the status bar said it was still searching for a signal. *Figures.* I powered it off and slumped in my seat.

Dad gave the horn another loud, long squawk. "You'd think for what we're paying they'd send someone out to greet us."

Mom shot back, "Maybe if you weren't so rude…"

Just then a horse and rider came galloping into view. The cowboy aimed his steed toward a hitching post, dismounted, and approached our vehicle with a slow, bow-legged stride.

"Howdy folks, I'm Wyatt Earp. You must be the Caden family."

"I'm Frank. This is my wife Sylvia and our youngest, Wendy."

The old man peered through Dad's open window in my direction. "And who's that handsome buckaroo back there?"

Buckaroo? Did he really call me a buckaroo?

Dad eyed me in the rearview mirror. "Nick."

"What's your pony's name?" I said to the old man.

Wyatt Earp glanced over his shoulder at the spotted horse. "Her? That's Marge. Named after my first wife. She was a nag too."

I cringed at his lame joke, refusing to give him the benefit of a smile.

"Hang this parkin' pass from your mirror," Earp said to Dad. "Follow this road over that rise and park behind Lazy Jack's. Someone'll come along shortly to meet you and unload your stuff. We got a stagecoach that will take you to your cabin."

"Did you hear that, Frank? A stagecoach. I don't remember reading anything about a stagecoach on the website."

"Website's sort of dated, ma'am. Owner's niece is supposed

to keep it up, but you know how it is with youngins these days," he said, eyeing me.

Yep. This is definitely going to be one of the worst vacations ever.

I returned to my gaming magazine. The reviewer had given *Deadly Encounters* two stars, noting its poor graphics and obvious clues.

"How old are you, son?"

As with all "who-done-it" murder mystery games, the article began, the key to solving the crime is discarding red herrings and keeping track of the suspects' means, motives, and opportunities to commit murder. Remember rule number one for sleuthing: The first suspect you meet is never the killer. Rule number two: Don't trust rule number one.

"Nick, Mr. Earp asked you a question."

"Fourteen," I answered without looking up.

"Say again?"

"One four."

"Annie's 'bout your age. That's the marshal's niece. Annie Oakley. Just her stage name. Real name is…well, can't recall right now but it'll come to me. Always does eventually. Two of you probably have a lot in common."

Doubt it.

Resting his elbow on the car roof, he leaned toward Dad as if the two of them were best buds. "You folks might want to keep an eye out for Black Bart. I hear tell someone saw him ride into town a few days ago. Haven't spotted him yet myself, but your boy there, being a young whippersnapper and all, he could get hurt if he came upon that outlaw unarmed."

Whippersnapper? Is this guy for real?

"Just 'tween you and me, I think he'll have more trouble with the grizzlies than gunslingers. Still, best to make sure he doesn't go wanderin' off."

"We understand," Mom answered.

Wyatt Earp reached through the window on Dad's side of the car and handed Dad our welcome packet, then waved us through. The gate arm had barely cleared the roof before Dad accelerated and sped off, startling a herd of horses grazing near the fence that ran alongside the drive. How many horses were there? Twenty? Fifty? I wondered how hard it would be to ride one. Or if they'd even let me.

I'll probably get a pony—with a helmet.

Dad parked beside Lazy Jack's Stable and we piled out. My attention was immediately drawn to the deep-throated roar of a high-performance engine. Jogging towards Lazy Jack's, I heard my sister whining, "Daaaaad! Nick's not helping!"

I rounded the corner and looked inside the barn. The yellow Dodge Charger sat parked at the far end of the barn, its hood poking out open bay doors. A black racing stripe ran from the rear to the hood, matching the black spoiler on the trunk. Chrome exhaust pipes peeked out from under the chassis, matching the glint of the eighteen-inch polished wheels. Dad was yelling something at me but his words became lost in the guttural growl of the Hemi's 425 horsepower, 6.1 liter engine.

The rumble of the engine ceased; the driver stepped out. For an instant I saw a blur of denim jeans and a checkered shirt before the driver slammed the car door shut and hurried around the corner of the barn and out of sight. I realized the car appeared similar if not identical to the one that had passed us coming up the mountain—the one Mom had said was driving too fast.

I walked toward the car, listening to the pinging sound of the cooling engine and inhaling the smell of exhaust. Mom called, "NICK! WE'RE WAITING!"

Shoving my hands in my pockets, I turned and started out of the barn but stopped abruptly when crimson drops splattered the sawdust next to my sneaker. Looking up I saw a smear of red on the rafters. Drip, drip, splat. Elongated drops quivered like dripping paint then fell, turning the beige sawdust a silky brown.

"NICK, THE STAGECOACH IS HERE. YOU COMING OR NOT?"

Ignoring Mom, I bolted toward the stairs, taking the steps two at a time and reaching the loft just as Dad laid on the horn. A young cowboy lay among the bales of hay, his curled fingers resting on his chest—a crimson stain slowly turning his white shirt into evidence.

Red blood cells emit a metallic odor. The smell comes from congealing hemoglobin as oxygen mixes with iron. The gunshot wound was fresh and bubbled like a gurgling geyser ready to erupt, only I knew with each popping bubble his blood pressure lessoned. He was leaking a lot.

With the toe of my sneaker I nudged his scuffed cowboy boot, half-expecting the body to sit up, grin a syrupy-red smile, and spit away plastic capsules. *This is a genuine Old West ghost town, right? Maybe part of the drill is to be greeted by a dead cowboy in the loft.*

I bumped him again and he didn't move.

Here's the thing about death that my parents don't get. Once you lose a couple of friends like I have, you become sort of numb to it. Like the first time, when my friend Teddy Graham got tossed from his mom's car, a bunch of us lit candles along the front walk of our school. I was pretty torn up about it, but I didn't cry. At least not around my classmates. Then a few weeks later a boy in my biology class smashed into a tree while snowboarding and died of brain injuries. It was like, "Okay, that's freaky." By the time spring rolled around, I'd lost two more classmates to freak accidents, but by then I just felt numb—like there was a big scab over my heart.

That's what I was thinking as I looked at that cowboy. That I should've been more upset than I was.

A whirring noise caught my attention. Stepping past the bales of hay, I saw a video of a grizzled gunslinger projected on the far wall. He stood with hands by his sides, right palm hovering on the hilt of a revolver. A wide-brim hat cast a shadow over his dark eyes. With his sun-browned face and thick black sideburns, he looked as real as the body behind me. It was obvious the video had been filmed in town. I recognized the saloon in the background.

Slowly the cowboy tilted his head and stared at me as if tracking my movements, making it feel as though he was with me in the loft. His hands hovered over the holstered guns, fingers twitching the way I'd seen in Dad's collection of Spaghetti Western movies. All that was missing was the hokey soundtrack. In a blur he drew and fired and ... vanished. The projector cycled off, leaving me alone to my morbid thoughts.

A horn honked. And honked. And honked. Dad's signal

that the waiting game was finished. I took a final glance at the dead cowboy's fixed eyes and bloody shirt and hurried down the steps, out of the barn, and toward the waiting stagecoach, certain of only one thing—this was going to be the best summer vacation ever.

CHAPTER TWO
AN INVITATION TO MURDER

"What do you mean there's a dead cowboy in the barn?"

Marshal Walter Buckleberry stood over me. Early forties, maybe older. Silver star above the left breast pocket of a khaki shirt. Pale gray eyes gazed down at me beneath the brim of a high-crown cowboy hat. I guessed him to be a few inches taller than Dad and pounds lighter. Shoulders and biceps filled his shirt nicely.

I gulped from a water bottle and replied, "Just what I said. Go look for yourself if you don't believe me."

The marshal held my gaze, refusing to break eye contact. We'd started off on the wrong foot and neither of us was going to apologize. At last, he looked away toward Lazy Jack's.

"What'd this fellow look like? This dead cowboy you *think* you saw?"

Sitting with my back against the stagecoach's wagon wheel, I described the way the blood gurgled from his chest and spread across the white shirt and how his bent fingers had formed a tent over the wound.

"Sounds like he's dead all right. What made you go in there in the first place?" the marshal asked me.

"Heard a car engine racing. Sounded like a supercharged Hemi with dual cams. Chrysler only offered that version on select models of the Charger. Can go from zero to sixty in six seconds. You can tell it's the stock supercharged model because of the Thrush mufflers. When I rounded the corner of the barn there she sat on Hoosier racing slicks. Yellow with a black racing stripe. Somebody around here's got an awesome ride."

"You sure that's the car you saw? Couldn't have been another make?"

"My son has a thing about automobiles," Dad interjected. "Has since he could crawl. First word was car."

"What about the driver? You say you saw him?"

"Could've been a her. Didn't see the face. Wore jeans and a tan and gold checkered shirt. If I'd arrived a few seconds earlier, I might have caught 'em in the act."

"So after this mysterious driver bolted from the barn you ran up the stairs and found the victim?" I chugged more water, nodding. "Is that when the dead cowboy vanished?"

"No, sir. The gunslinger in the video disappeared. Dead man's still there."

"Boss! Might have something." Another officer hurried over and held out his palm. "Found this in the wall."

Buckleberry eyed the smashed slug and asked, "And the victim?"

The deputy glanced at me, then back at the marshal. "No body, boss. No blood, neither."

"What do you mean?" the marshal said, fixing his gaze on me again. "Boy here says he saw a man get shot."

"*Found* him," I corrected. "Didn't actually witness the murder."

"There's a set of sneaker prints in the sawdust," the deputy replied, pointing toward my shoes. "But nothing else. No, wait. I forgot something. I found Jess's car parked in there."

"I'm telling you, Marshal. There's a dead man in that barn." Tossing my water bottle aside, I added, "If you'll just come with me ..."

Marshal Buckleberry's face softened. "Relax, son. No one is accusing you of making up stuff. But this *is* a ghost town. Not everything you'll see over the next few days is what it seems."

"I know what I saw, Marshal. And it wasn't a ghost."

"Tell you what. Why don't you folks get checked into your rooms," the marshal said to Mom and Dad. "I'll walk over to the barn and see if I can find out where our dead cowboy wandered off to. If he's shot like your boy says, he couldn't have gone too far."

"Want me to go with you, boss? Help you look?"

The marshal rounded on the deputy and said flatly, "One of us ought to be enough. Just bag that slug and put it in my saddlebag. I'll send it to the lab in Denver. Maybe they can pull something off it."

Marshal Buckleberry waited until his deputy was out of

earshot before saying to my parents, "Man knows better than to remove evidence from a crime scene without gloves. Ought to write him up, but I just plain don't have the time to fill out the paperwork. Imagine if there *had* been a murder."

I stood, brushing dirt off the back of my jeans.

"But there *was*."

Dad cut in. "I hate to ask the obvious, but is it possible my son is telling the truth?"

The marshal rubbed a knuckle against his chin and smiled at me. "Son, here's what I *think* you saw. Tell me when I go off track. The man you say got shot, he was young, not much older than you. Slight build, blue eyes, buck-toothed smile. Wore a big square black hat with a band around the base. Yellow bandana around his neck. How am I doing?"

"That's him! That's the victim!"

Buckleberry turned toward my parents. "Name's Billy the Kid. Nasty one. Hot tempered. Quick on the draw too. At least that's the role he plays in our little performance. Real name is Billy Bell. An actor out of Los Angeles. Had a bit roll in that teen movie, *The Boy Next Door*. Now he's up for a supporting role in the remake of *Rio Bravo*."

"Any idea why someone would want him dead?" I asked.

Buckleberry chuckled. "Trying to do my job for me?"

"Maybe the dead guy *is* a ghost," my sister said sarcastically. "Ever think of that, Nick?"

"No such thing as ghosts," I answered.

Balling her fists on her hips, she snapped back. "Oh yes there is."

My sister is at that age where she'll believe almost anything except what I tell her. I have friends with younger siblings and they're always complaining about how their little sisters and brothers follow them around, treating them like they're some sort of god. Not Wendy. She's the *older* sister I'm glad I never had.

"Just because *you* believe in vampires, werewolves, and witches," I replied, "doesn't mean they're real." I turned toward the marshal. "I know what I saw. And I'm telling you, there's a dead man in that barn. Or was."

The marshal pushed his hat back on his head and said to me, "Look, son. We work hard to make sure our guests have a good time. If we weren't such good actors no one would bother to drive all the way out here. I'm sure this isn't the only shoot-out you'll witness while in Deadwood. There's lots of dangerous folks in this territory. Bank bandits and train robbers and hired guns, like Black Bart, just itching for a fight."

"Guard at the gate mentioned him," Mom chimed in.

"But to put your mind at ease, I'll poke around in the barn. Could be my deputy missed something. In the meantime I'd suggest you folks head on to the bunkhouse. It'll be dark soon. Past few weeks we've had brown bears rummaging around in the garbage. Got a call into the Department of Wildlife, but they haven't done anything about it yet."

"You didn't answer my question," I said. "Who *benefits* if Billy the Kid is dead?"

Sighing heavily, Buckleberry stared at the snow-capped peaks glowing orange from the setting sun. "Let's just say Bill isn't the most popular employee in Deadwood. Sort of has it in his head he's better than the other actors. And maybe he is. We're lucky he's hung around as long as he has. But I can't imagine anyone wanting to kill him."

Taking the reins of his horse, the marshal stepped one foot into the stirrups and swung himself into the saddle.

"Look, you seem like fine people. My advice is to forget about all this business in the hayloft and get washed up for dinner. Sassy Sally's Saloon serves a fine meal. I'm partial to the beef barbeque sandwich, but their chili is good too. I think if you'll check your schedule you'll see there's a buffalo hunt scheduled early in the morning. You're not going to want to miss that. Know what I mean?"

"Don't worry, Marshal. I'll make sure my son doesn't go snooping around that barn in the dark."

"You do that, Mr. Caden."

I watched Marshal Buckleberry ride toward the barn, dismount, and enter Lazy Jack's. I wanted to run over and see for myself if the body was gone but before I could ask Dad if I could, my sister quipped, "Way to go, Nick. We haven't even had time to unpack and the marshal is already threatening to ride us out of town."

"For once, why can't you just do like you're asked?" Mom added.

"Would the two of you cut him some slack?" said Dad. "I'm sure Nick will be on his best behavior now, won't you, son?"

"I know what I saw, Dad. And it wasn't a ghost. Or some video of a fake gunfight." Grabbing my backpack from the pile of bags tossed onto the roof of the stagecoach, I flung open the door and slid across the seat as far as I could. The setting sun began to turn the mountains pink. Slanting rays crept across

the pasture, casting long rooftop shadows. *Was it a cheap parlor trick? A clever act?* I could see how video of the gunslinger might be part of the ghost town theatrics. But the dead man? He was real; I was sure of it.

Can't fake the metallic smell of blood.

While Dad chatted with the stagecoach driver and Wendy patted the horses, I unzipped the front compartment of my backpack and grabbed my gaming magazine. *Might as well finish reading the review*, I thought.

I opened the magazine; a barroom napkin landed in my lap. Stamped across the front was a colorful sketch of Sassy Sally's Saloon. On the back a personalized message addressed to me.

IF YOU WANT TO CATCH MY KILLER, BE AT BOOT HILL THIS EVENING. MIDNIGHT. It was signed, Billy the Kid.

CHAPTER THREE
DEAD MAN'S HAND

I left my bags on the floor of what passed for the Bat Masterson Suite (one bunk, one sink with cold water, dripping shower faucet) and returned to the front porch of our bunkhouse. The clapboard building was painted a violent shade of yellow, its tin roof fireball red. The sky had turned a brilliant orange and there was a perceptible chill in the air. In the open field that linked the bunkhouses, a heavy-set father tossed logs onto a campfire while his boys played horseshoes.

I dropped into a rocker and propped my sneakers onto the rough-hewn porch railing. It occurred to me that any number of people could have killed the actor Bill Bell. The white-haired security guard, Wyatt Earp, hadn't been at his post when we'd arrived. Maybe Dad's horn honking had interrupted him before he could dispose of the body. Marshal Buckleberry. He and his deputy had seemed to arrive out of nowhere. Had I stumbled upon a heated argument gone bad? Wouldn't be the first time a law enforcement officer was involved in a cover-up.

Then there was the mysterious driver of the sports car, the one dressed in jeans and a checkered shirt who looked eerily like the phantom figure I'd seen in the hayloft. I thought back to our ride up the mountain and how Mom had complained about the speeding Dodge Charger zooming past us in the middle of a blind turn. Same car? And if it was, would the driver have arrived ahead of us in time to kill Billy the Kid before I charged into the barn?

"How's your room?" Wendy stood behind me holding open the screen door. "I have a fireplace in mine. Bet yours doesn't have a fireplace. I'm in the Calamity Jane room. Did you know her real name was Martha Jane Cannary Burke? Says so right here on the brochure. I think I heard Mom say they're in the Annie Oakley suite. Did you know she's really here, Annie Oakley? Pamphlet calls her a 'dead-eye marksman.'"

I said nothing. Just kept staring at the campfire and watching the two boys thump the grass with horseshoes.

"Mom says we're walking up as soon as she gets out of the shower. Dinner in a saloon—is that awesome or what?"

"Oughta be a real hootenanny."

"Gee, Nick. You could at least *pretend* like you're having a good time."

"Did you see anyone come out of Lazy Jack's after I went in? Or come around the side of the building?"

"You mean while we were loading our stuff onto the roof of the stagecoach? No, why?"

I pushed myself up from my rocker. "Think I'll wander into town. See if I can get a cell connection. I think we're in a dead zone," I remarked, waving at the cluster of trees flanking the creek. "Tell Mom and Dad I'll be in the saloon."

"You're not going to try to sneak back into that barn, are you?"

"You think I should?" I caught her glaring at me. "Relax, sis. I won't do anything stupid." She hates it when I call her sis. And I hate being tattled on by my younger sister. "If I stumble into a brown bear I'll take a picture with my phone and save it for you."

The heavy aroma of fried food greeted me as I stepped through the swinging doors of Sassy Sally's. Men and women leaned against the bar, elbow to elbow, boots hooked on bar-rungs. Cowboy hats and overcoats hung on dowels. Guests sat around square tables and feasted on fried chicken, corn on the cob, and steaming bowls of beans. A piano player banged away at a riveting rendition of "Yellow Rose of Texas." On the far side of the saloon, card players sat hunched forward and tossed wooden chips onto the green felt.

I slid onto a bar stool. "Is there any place around here I can get a decent cell signal?" The bartender, a whiskered man with hound-dog eyes and oily bangs, dried a shot glass.

I held up my phone. "You know? Talkie, talkie?"

The bartender slapped his towel over his shoulder and wad-
dled off to take another drink order.

"General store has a pay phone," said Marshal Buckleberry,
sidling up next to me. "And if you need to get online, you're
welcome to borrow my computer. I have dial-up."

Dial-up? You kidding me? Smoke signals would be faster.

"But the best advice I can give you is to just relax and forget
texting and talking and checking your email while you're here.
One of the best parts of Deadwood is that we're a long ways
from no place."

"So no cell coverage," I answered. "Not even a little?"

"Closest tower is two miles west of Rattlesnake Gulch. If
you catch the wind right you might get one bar."

"Rattlesnake, that's...?"

"A place you'll want to avoid, for obvious reasons. By the
way, I checked the barn like I promised. Found the Charger,
but no body or blood."

"Marshal, I'm telling you, a man died in that hayloft. As a
law enforcement officer, I'd think you'd be concerned."

He popped a handful of peanuts into his mouth and chased
it with a shot of what I guessed to be tea made to look like
whiskey.

Aiming those tired gray eyes in my direction, Marshal
Buckleberry said, "What makes you think you're qualified to
judge what I should and shouldn't be concerned about?"

"Solving murders is sort of a hobby of mine."

"That so." He scooped another fist of nuts. "Well? Tell me
about this hobby."

"Actually, it's more than a hobby. A bunch of us formed

this association called Cybersleuths. We use online investigative tools to examine real murders and solve cases."

Marshal Buckleberry raised his eyebrows. "Really? What sort of tools?"

Looking away, I studied the poker players across the room. "Television detective shows, mostly."

"Say again?"

"I watch crime shows and compare those crimes against actual murders."

Choking on the nuts, the marshal drained his drink. "Well, that's a new one."

"It's not as crazy as it sounds, Marshal. The way it works is, after we've gathered all the data from a real crime, I run a versatile statistical analysis algorithm for the detection of aberrations."

"You do what to who?"

"Check for trends that might hint as to who committed the murder and why. A lot of what you see on television is pure fiction. Just stuff the show's producer tosses in for dramatic effect. But sometimes you find an episode where they've used a real crime scene expert as a consultant. That can be useful. Once I have the final report of all the suspects, their motives, means, and opportunities, I load that into a database. But it's not just me working on the cases. There's a whole group of us. Together we check the real crimes against television shows that have similar elements. Each member of our group has a special area of interest. I'm a huge *NCIS* and *Criminal Minds* fan."

"I can't imagine that anyone could ever solve a murder doing something as silly as that."

"Actually, it's a lot easier than you think. Our analysis usually renders a fairly accurate summary of who the likely perpetrator is. The good news is, most murders are committed by really dumb people, so finding the killer isn't as hard as most people imagine."

"Sounds like you got it all figured out. Don't hardly see where you even need my help finding Billy the Kid's killer. But just to be safe, I wouldn't go around talking too much about what you think you saw. Folks might not take too kindly to you accusing them of murder."

He cut his eyes across the room toward the poker table. A new player had joined the game and sat with his back to me. He wore a checkered shirt similar to the one worn by the driver of the Dodge Charger. Same color pants, too.

"Now if you'll excuse me," the marshal said, patting his vest pocket, "I got to get this slug off to ballistics."

When Mom and Dad arrived, I joined them in the buffet line.

"Nick, make sure you get some vegetables," Mom said, chiding me on my lousy eating habits. "You know what the doctor said about your cholesterol level."

I waited until she'd moved down the line before dumping two spoonfuls of mashed potatoes on my plate and snagging a roll.

"That's not a vegetable," Wendy quipped.

"And you're not my mother."

"Mom! Nick said he's not—"

I spooned a small helping of green beans onto my plate. "There, happy?"

My sister smirked. I plopped another, larger helping onto *her* buttered roll and pushed past her.

"I think that's him," I said, sliding into the chair next to Dad. "That guy at the poker table is the person I saw getting out of the car."

"Thought you said you didn't see his face."

"I didn't, but he's wearing the same outfit."

Taking a cue from another player, the mysterious card player hooked his arm on his chair and pivoted, staring at me. Same black hat with the low crown, same thick sideburns as the phantom figure in the hayloft. With his gaze still locked on me, the gunslinger aimed his finger at me and pretended to squeeze the trigger.

"That's him!" I whispered to Dad. "That's the guy I saw in the hayloft."

"The dead man?"

"No! The man in the video. *And* getting out of the Charger."

"Don't murderers usually flee the scene of a crime?" my sister said sarcastically. "Or maybe it's different for ghosts."

"What about ghosts?" said Mom, walking back from the dessert bar.

"Nick thinks he sees one."

"Really? Where?"

"That's not what I said."

"That's what I *heard*."

Mom paused from unloading her tray and scanned the room. "Where is the ghost?"

I pointed toward the poker table.

"Looks like a bunch of men playing poker to me," Mom said, sounding disappointed.

"Nick thinks that might be the guy he saw in the video," Dad said to Mom.

"And in the car," I added.

"Well for gosh sakes, don't say or do anything to upset him, Nicholas. This isn't a game like your online detective group. You can't just walk up to people and question them about a murder."

"I *know* that, Mom. But I would like to ask him where he was earlier this evening."

"And if he was in the barn?" Dad replied.

"I don't know, Nick. That guy looks like a real outlaw," Wendy said, mocking me. "What if he draws on you?"

"Maybe I'll drag you over there and use you for cover."

"Would you two stop?" said Mom. "People are starting to stare."

"Son, pass the salt."

"Frank, you know what the doctor said."

"And the butter," Dad added.

"I'll be right back," I said, pushing back my chair.

Mom grabbed my wrist. "Sit!"

"Yeah, Nick." Wendy waved an ear of corn at me. "Haven't you caused enough trouble already?"

The din of chatter stopped abruptly. Everyone turned to watch a gaunt farmer wearing a stained long-john shirt and mud-splattered pants step away from the poker table.

Clearing his throat the farmer said to the mysterious card player, "You haven't lost a hand since you got the deal. If I didn't know better, I'd say you's cheatin'."

The man from the hayloft stopped shuffling. Without

looking up he said, "Then I reckon it's a good thing you know better than to say a thing like that."

"Maybe I don't," the farmer replied. "Maybe you is cheating. Maybe you's a lyin' card shark who's dealing off the bottom."

"Watch your mouth, hayseed."

"How 'bout you watch your'n. And how 'bout pay me back what you stole?" The farmer's right hand hovered over his gun, fingers trembling.

The other players pushed away from the table, scattering for cover. The room fell deathly silent.

With his head still bowed, the accused man snarled, "I don't cheat."

"I says different."

"I don't cheat!"

"Then how is it you been dealing yourself doubles and straights since you sat down?"

"Lucky streak, I guess."

"And I says that streak just ended. Ain't that right, fellows?" The farmer looked around nervously, searching the crowd for support.

The man stood slowly, turning toward the farmer. "Walk away, hayseed. No point getting killed over a few lousy hands of cards."

The farmer widened his stance, his eyes tracking the gun-fighter's movements. "Can't. Not 'til you give back what you took from me."

"This is so cool," Wendy said in a low voice. "Just like in the movies."

Dad leaned over and asked me, "You sure it's him?"

"I … think so. But he looks different somehow. Not sure why."

"Probably because he has skin on," Wendy snarked.

The gunfighter eased sideways, crabbing away from the table, until the two men faced each other in the middle of the saloon.

"You don't want to draw on Jesse James," announced the piano player. "He'll kill ya."

The farmer's eyebrows arched. "J-J-Jesse James … I … had no idea," he stammered.

"Simple mistake. Now walk on."

For a moment I thought he might. I would. The guy in the video, this Jesse James, had the look of a deadly gunslinger.

The farmer shot a glance toward the green felt cloth and the pile of cash and chips on the table, then squared his shoulders. "No sir, I can't. Way I see it, I just plain don't have any choice but to get back what's mine."

Jesse James's brow furrowed. "Man's always got a choice. You get the first move, hayseed. I owe you that."

The farmer's hand flinched but never reached the holster.

The revolver's muzzle blast came so quick it was over before I had a chance to blink. Stumbling backwards, the farmer's face twisted in pain. He took a half step toward our table and dropped face down, making no attempt to break his fall. For a few seconds he laid there, blood pooling around his body and soaking the sides of his threadbare long-john shirt. Then, his shape changed, becoming less defined and more… translucent. I leaned forward, we all did, and watched as the farmer vanished—body, bloodstain, and all!

Jesse James holstered his gun and surveyed the crowd, his

dark eyes settling on me. With a derisive sneer he turned and exited the saloon, slipping out a side door.

"Did you see that?" shrieked Wendy. "That was so awesome."

"Trapdoor," Dad said. "Has to be. No way that farmer was a video image. He was too real. Bet if we look we can find where the hinges are sunk into the wood."

"Told you it was all an act," Wendy said to me. "And you fell for it. Some great detective you are."

But I hardly heard my sister because I was already halfway across the saloon. I slammed my shoulder into the door and burst into the alley, looking left, then right. No Jesse James. No one at all except the person pressing the barrel of a gun against my temple.

"One wrong move and you die."

CHAPTER FOUR
DEPUTIZED

"Scared you, didn't I?" the young woman said.

I felt her remove the gun from my head and turned. In the ambient light of dusk I made a quick assessment. *My height, my age. Reddish-blonde bangs and ponytail. Freckled cheeks under the pale sombrero. Not bad looking, even though the revolver in her hand is a huge turn off.*

I said, "Would you please put that thing away?"

"Is it making you uncomfortable?"

"Yes, a little."

"See that sign?" She gestured toward a wooden notice mounted on a post at the entrance to the alley. TRESPASSERS SHOT ON SITE. "Means you can't be out here."

"Shouldn't that be 'sight'?" I asked.

"You know what it means," she said, tucking the gun into its holster. The blue denim shirt fit the rough and tumbleweed tomboy look but did little to suppress the more pronounced features of her cowgirl frame.

"S-i-t-e means a place, location," I explained. "S-i-g-h-t has to do with vision."

"All I know is you're not supposed to be out here. We have a strict policy. No one allowed on the back lot."

"You're here."

"I work here, Jethro."

"Name's Nick."

"I *know* what your name is. Uncle Walt's told me all about you."

"Uncle Walt?"

"Marshal Buckleberry."

The niece in charge of maintaining the out-of-date website. Probably in charge of signage too.

I said, "Aren't you a little young to be a peace officer?"

"Bet I'm older than you."

"Doubt it. I turn fifteen next month."

Beaming, she announced, "Me too. What day?"

I pointed to the revolver on her hip. "Is that thing loaded?"

"Need a permit to carry a loaded weapon and I don't have one. Impressive, isn't it? Replica of a Colt Six-Shooter. Fires 9 mm blanks as fast as you can cock the hammer. Here, try it out."

Before I could tell her I wasn't interested, she moved next to me and took my right wrist, placing the gun in my hand.

Together we raised the weapon slowly. "Now, aim at something and—"

The sound of the gun blast startled me. Quickly, she thumbed back the hammer, readying it again. "Block out the distractions," she said, her cheek nearly touching mine, "and you'll hit the target every time."

"But it's shooting blanks."

"Still doesn't hurt to practice."

She curled her fingers over my hand and I realized how uncomfortable I felt standing so close to her.

Cooing into my ear she said, "Now, try again."

The saloon door flung open and we untangled ourselves.

Marshal Buckleberry stepped out. "What's going on out here?"

Taking the weapon from me, the young woman returned the revolver to its holster. "Just showing this clodhopper how we do things in Deadwood."

"You know better than to let a guest handle your sidearm. Now get back inside and help bus those tables."

"That's what the kitchen staff is for."

"For crying out loud, Annie. For once would you just do what I ask you to do without arguing?"

"Fine," she said, yanking open the door. "But if Mom was here she wouldn't make me—"

"Inside!"

"Seventeenth," she called over her shoulder. "My birthday is the seventeenth."

"Got you by three days," I answered.

"You haven't got me at all, Nick Caden. Not by a long

shot." The door banged shut, leaving me alone in the alley with the marshal.

"If I were you, son, I'd steer clear of my niece. She's a brush fire in a dry wind."

"That brush fire got a name?"

"Annie. Annabel Nora Lancaster. Named after my sister, God rest her soul. But now she calls herself Annie Oakley."

"Like the Old West exhibition shooter?"

"Exactly like that." The marshal jabbed his thumb back toward the door. "So tell me. What'd you think of our little gunfight in there? Look familiar?"

"The body in the barn didn't disappear, Marshal, but I can see why you'd think I was mistaken. That's a good act, making the farmer vanish like that. What I want to know is how you could rig a trapdoor in a hayloft."

"I checked the barn like I said I would and didn't find a sign of foul play. Guess that makes me a pretty lousy lawman."

"Somebody could've moved the body before you and your deputy had a chance to look. Like, maybe the driver of the Dodge Charger."

"You mean Jess? Doubtful. He was already preparing for the saloon scene. Makes more sense that there never was a body."

"I'm going back inside," I said. "My parents are probably wondering what happened to me."

The marshal put his hand on the door, pushing it shut. "Look, son. We work hard to keep our guests entertained. Maybe too hard. But people drive a long way to get here, and they expect to get a real taste of the Old West."

"You have a killer running loose, Marshal. I doubt that's the ghost town experience they bargained for."

"Walk with me," he said. "I want to show you something."

I followed him down the alley and beyond the clatter coming from behind the kitchen's screen door. A trash receptacle had been painted to look like a wooden water barrel, but the sour odor of spoiled milk and rotten food destroyed the illusion.

"What you have to understand is that tourism is a competitive industry," the marshal continued. "Hard to compete with those theme parks. Kids these days want fast and scary with lots of things exploding and flying around. But I don't have to tell you this. Bet you weren't all that excited when your mom and dad picked Deadwood for their vacation."

We turned down a side street bracketed by a livery stable, blacksmith shop, and tannery. In the distance I spied a corral and beyond, the rutted path of a wagon trail.

I said, "If it had been up to me, we'd have gone to Vegas. There's a gaming convention out there. My sister lobbied for Disney World but Dad said he wasn't going to spend that kind of money to stand in line for hours with a bunch of bawling babies in strollers. Mom said as long as we all agreed on the destination, she didn't care where we went. I didn't agree to come here, but obviously no one pays much attention to what I say."

"Family vacations were different when I was your age. Dad would load up the station wagon and we'd all pile in, stop at the filling station for gas and to check the oil, then we'd head off on Route 66. Back then you could actually stop on the side of the highway, spread a blanket, and have a picnic. We'd eat my mother's deviled eggs and fried chicken and drink sodas out of a glass bottle. Got a nickel a piece for those bottles when

I turned them in. Now it's kids listening to music through their headphones or watching videos on their smart phones while mom reads and dad navigates interstate traffic. For me to convince a family that it's worth their time to come all the way out here and spend a few days looking up at the stars and relaxing is a tough sell."

If the marshal was trying to make me feel sorry for him, it wasn't working.

We covered the three blocks from the saloon to the corral, walking past the rear of the general store, hotel, and the town's lone church—a compact white structure with a prominent steeple. We hooked a left at a feed store and approached a modular trailer sitting on sturdy cinder block supports. Buckleberry took a ring of keys from his belt and unlocked the door, motioning me inside.

"My office," he said, flipping on an overhead fluorescent light.

The trailer had the strong odor of new carpet. Beige walls, beige carpet, brown desk. He pointed toward a straight-back wooden chair. "Sit." Boxes lined the baseboards. A floor vent exhaled warm air. He pulled open the top drawer of a filing cabinet, removed a folder, and began scribbling something on a sheet of paper.

"I expected the marshal's office would have jail cells," I said, tipping the chair onto its rear legs. "And a hat rack covered with ten-gallon hats."

"*That* office is on the other end of Main Street." He pushed the sheet of paper inside a manila envelope and sealed the flap. "This is my real office." Opening another folder, he scribbled more notes, causing the gold tassel of a green lamp atop the filing cabinet to jiggle. Slamming the file cabinet shut, he dropped into a worn leather chair and spun to face me from across the desk.

"We have a problem, you and me."

I stared at him, unsure of what he meant.

"See, if someone goes around saying they've witnessed a murder, even a kid with an overactive imagination, it could be bad for business. Normally I wouldn't mind the publicity. Even bad press is better than none. But I don't want the guests to get so worked up about some make-believe murder they don't have a good time. Understand what I'm saying?"

"Well ... sure. I don't want to spread rumors that aren't true, either. But there *is* a killer. Or was."

"See? That's exactly the sort of talk I'm worried about." Linking his hands behind his head he leaned back in his chair. "I've been thinking how we might help each other."

I studied his face, wondering where he was going with this.

"I got a bumbling deputy who might have botched an investigation. Don't think he did, 'cause like I said, I have no reason to think there's been a crime committed. But from the looks of things, you seem determined to keep meddling."

He paused, allowing his words to sink in.

"I spoke with your parents back there in the saloon about that television detective thing you told me about. Your dad claims you're pretty good. I have to tell you, most of what you said back there made no sense to me. Database algorithms and parsing case files. Stuff is way over my head. But your parents made it clear that they want you to have a good time while you're in Deadwood, so I've been thinking how you and me can come to an agreement."

"What sort of agreement?"

"What if I was to deputize you? In a temporary capacity?"

I searched those pale gray wolf eyes, waiting for the punch line that didn't come.

"Why would you do that?" I asked. "You don't even believe me."

"Like I said, my deputy might have missed something. The truth is, neither of us has much experience with this sort of thing. I spent a few years on the force but never investigated a murder. And the only law enforcement experience Gabrovski ever got involved standing guard while police investigated a home invasion."

"Gabrovski?"

"Deputy Pat Garrett. That's his stage name. His real name is Patrick Gabrovski. Ran a small home-security firm before I hired him on. Lucky I did too. Had just about lost all his clients."

"So you want me to do your detective work for you?"

"Like I said before, I don't think there's a crime to investigate. But if someone was killed and you're as good as your mom and dad think you are, maybe you'll find something we missed."

Deputy marshal in an Old West ghost town. Didn't see that coming. I said, "What's the catch?"

"You stop telling everyone there's a killer running loose until you can prove otherwise."

"I'll need to get on the Internet. Something faster than that dial-up."

He held up a blue ethernet cable. "I was just messing with you. Don't want folks traipsing in here all day asking to check their email. You can use my computer. Of course, I'll need to be with you when you do. So do we have a deal?"

"Well sure, I guess." I didn't know if I should stand and shake his hand, so instead I said, "You had something you wanted to show me?"

"Right. Not so much show as hear." He punched buttons on the desk phone and hit the speaker button. There was beeping, then a man's voice.

"Sorry to call so late, Marshal. It's been a madhouse out here. And every time I thought to ring you, they'd call me back on the set. Crazy fun but I swear by the time I hit the sack it's time to get up again. Right, I'm rambling like always. Day before yesterday…no, must've been the day before that, I got a call from the studio. The producer says he wants to begin filming right away. I told him no way. That I had to clear it with you first and besides, I couldn't get a flight out in time. He says I'm either on the set the next morning or they're giving the part to another actor. You and I both know who he meant."

I started to ask but the marshal held up his hand, silencing me.

"I took a chance you wouldn't be too sore. How I got to the airport without getting a ticket I'll never know. Caught a flight to Phoenix and a connecting to LAX. Anyway, I'm calling to let you know I won't make it to work tonight. Or for a while. Hope that doesn't jam you up too much."

The voice mail ended.

Buckleberry smiled.

"Billy the Kid?" I offered.

"Call came in around the time you said you were in the barn looking at him bleeding to death. Now I'm no expert on television detective shows like you, but it seems to me it'd be hard for a victim to be two places at once unless maybe he was a ghost, which we both know he isn't."

"I don't know who that is on the phone, but it's not the man I saw in the hayloft."

"Tell you what, son. How 'bout tomorrow after the buffalo hunt, you and I take a look in that barn to see what we can find. How's that sound?"

"Fine. I guess."

He opened the top drawer and tossed a silver star onto the desk.

"Welcome to Deadwood, Deputy Nick Caden."

CHAPTER FIVE
A GRAVE DISCOVERY ON BOOT HILL

At half past eleven the alarm chirped on my phone, jarring me awake. The corner porch light outside my window cast yellow highlights across the ribbed slats of the empty bunk above my head. I sat up, cringing at the sound of creaking bedsprings. In the adjoining room, Dad's snoring momentarily stopped. I sat silently, legs dangling over the side of the bed. A coyote howled in the distant hills. The light on my phone dimmed just as Dad's locomotive exhalations resumed. I quickly wedged my feet into my sneakers and thumbed the latch on the window.

Clouds moved over a crescent moon, snuffing out stars. In the distance a low ridge at the base of the mountain range jutted skyward, forming a dark backdrop against the silhouette of rooftops and a church steeple. I slipped on my hooded sweat-shirt, placed my palms on the windowsill, and swung my legs out, dropping into dense weeds. Unfolding the map from my back pocket, I used my phone's screen to illuminate the route from our bunkhouse to Boot Hill.

The marshal's willingness to deputize me had been a favor to my parents. I could imagine Dad saying, "Humor him, Marshal. The boy's fourteen and bored." Regardless of what I did, no matter how many cases I solved *before* the authorities arrested the culprit, my parents still saw my amateur detective work as a hobby and me as their little boy—even if I was almost as tall as Dad.

When I reached town, I circled around the back of the saloon, taking the route Marshal Buckleberry used on his way to the office. Near a rack of trash bins came the sound of rustling and clanging, but when I peered back, the noise stopped. *Cat? Coyote? Bear?* Moving with more urgency, I followed the back road out of town past adobe huts advertising (in large letters, the misspelling clearly visible in my phone's lighted screen) AWTHINTIC NATIVE AMERICAN CRAFTS FOR SELL. The road wound around a cluster of large teepees before turning off into a field of scrub brush, cactuses, and small trees. At last I came to a dry riverbed. Large boulders lay scattered about. I aimed the screen of my phone at a sign nailed to a tree. WELCOME TO BOOT HILL: NO FIREARMS A LOUD.

A loud? You kidding me?

My amused reaction at yet another misspelling was interrupted by the sound of heavy breathing coming from the bushes ahead of me. I dropped into a crouch, unsure of what I'd do if the noise proved to be a bear. All I could remember from my quick online research in preparation for the trip was that bears could weigh as much as seventeen hundred pounds, and because they were too heavy to climb trees, they often attacked in defense of their territory.

The labored breathing grew louder. I slunk behind a scrawny pine, wishing I'd brought a bell or whistle or my dirt bike. A bulky figure took shape in the shadows, its massive haunch pushing past pine branches. *Six feet, at least. And that's on all fours!* I rose onto the balls of my feet, ready to bolt and knowing that even if I did, I was a dead man. No way I could outrun a beast like that.

The snapping of twigs and animal sounds intensified. The beast paused in a clearing and lifted its head as though sniffing the air for prey.

"What are you doing out here?"

Her voice, coming so close, sent my heart to pounding in my chest. I whirled to find the girl from the alley standing a few feet behind me.

"I could ask you the same thing," I shot back, still trying to tamp down the panic.

"Uncle Walt said I should keep an eye on you." She walked into the clearing, took the horse by the reins and tied it to a sturdy pine. "What are we looking for?"

"We?"

"You thinking of sneaking into the graveyard?"

"Keep your voice down," I said.

"Relax, there's no one around. I checked." She'd changed

from her western attire into jeans, a jacket, and hiking boots. She nodded toward a series of large boulders. "Planning on using *that* trail?"

"Is there another way to the graveyard?"

"No. But it can be tricky." She stepped past me. "And dangerous. I better go first."

The route—less a trail and more of a goat path—zigged and zagged up the steep grade. Annie scampered along with bobcat quickness, soon leaving me far behind. I wondered how anyone could carry a casket up such a rocky trail, but then maybe Boot Hill was like everything else in this dead town—for show only. After carefully working our way along a slope of loose, pellet-sized dirt, we reached a flat area about thirty yards wide and nearly as long. A single gnarled tree stood in the middle of the graveyard among weathered headstones. The markers jutted up from the ground like broken teeth, forming a snaggletooth grin.

"What now, Deputy?"

I studied her smile in the emerging moonlight. "We'll hide in those rocks at the base of that cliff."

Tall, wet weeds slapped against my pant legs as I walked through the gate of a wrought iron fence toward the bunker of rocks tumbled together at the base of the cliff. The sheer rock face rose several stories above us and formed the western flank of a mesa that overlooked the town.

"You're not worried about being trapped up here without a way out?"

"I don't expect to be seen," I said, squeezing past her.

I worked my way around the maze of jumbled rocks and

finally settled on a place behind two round boulders. From the gap between the rocks, I could see the rows of headstones, a tilting fence, and the trailhead upon which we had climbed.

"What about me?" Annie asked, trying to push her way close.

"You watch from the other end. And don't talk so much," I whispered. "We may not be alone."

Annie took a position about ten feet away, just under a low shelf that protruded from the cliff. She had to squat to remain hidden by the moon's shadow. I felt confident she wouldn't be seen. I peeked at my phone. Two minutes 'til twelve. I blew into my hands, warming my fingers.

"Your birthday really the fourteenth?" she asked in a strained whisper.

"You need to stop talking."

"We should friend each other."

"Hush!"

A sliver of yellow moon emerged from behind the clouds. Nearby an owl hooted. I kept my eyes fixed on the trailhead, refusing to look to my left even as I heard the sound of Annie shuffling in my direction. Gradually I became aware of her warmth next to me. In school I almost never stood this close to a girl. In the cafeteria line, sometimes, but this was different. I found myself listening to her breathing, watching her heated breaths congealing into fists of gray mist as the cool air settled upon us. I still wasn't sure how she'd known I would be at Boot Hill. Sure, she *could* have followed me. Maybe it'd been her I heard banging into the trash bins back in town. But it made more sense that she'd planted the note. Question was, when would she have had time? She hadn't been at the stagecoach when we'd arrived, and my knapsack hadn't been out of my sight except when Mom and Dad and Wendy were unloading the car and I was in Lazy Jack's. Unless she was the one I'd seen exiting the barn. *But what are the odds that she and Jesse James wear the same type of shirt?*

On the other side of the graveyard, rocks skittered away. Footsteps approached. Our hideout suddenly seemed small and exposed. Annie sucked in a breath, tensing up. She looped her arm into mine, and with our faces close together, we peered out across the graveyard.

"Listen, if anything happens," I whispered, "I want you to run back to town as fast as you can and get your uncle."

Annie hugged my arm tighter and said nothing.

A dark figure appeared, slowly moving through the gate toward the lone tree. He led a horse by the reins, the clomping of hooves muffling our own excited breathing. Looping the reins over a low branch, the stranger struck a match against the side of his boot and lit a small camping lantern. The mantle swelled, growing bright and illuminating the yellow bandana covering the lower half of his face.

"Is that him? The guy you saw in the barn?"

I clamped my hand over her mouth.

The man—and I felt confident it was a man—strolled past the first row of graves and paused, making a slow three-sixty turn before stomping down the weeds and carefully placing the lantern on the matted area. Once more he hesitated as if listening. I knew he heard my heart beating. A base drum would've made less noise. Annie nibbled on my finger. I removed my hand from her mouth.

"Don't you ever do that again," she hissed.

"Then please be quiet."

The man approached his horse and fiddled with cords and knots and, dropping into a half crouch, rolled something long and as large as a man's body onto his shoulder. Staggering under the weight, he walked back toward the lantern and dumped the heavy object onto the grass. In the glow of the lantern I could almost make out the shape of a head and shoulders pressing against the black plastic.

"Oh, this is bad," Annie said, her voice shaking. "When Uncle Walt said you witnessed a murder, I thought he was kidding."

"Will you pleeeease stop talking," I said, my voice barely audible.

The stranger walked back to his horse and returned with a collapsible shovel. I guessed the recent rains had made the ground soft because within minutes the man had dug a shallow trench. He leaned on the handle and, using the shovel like a fulcrum, rolled the body into the grave.

"If we hurry we can reach his horse before he can," Annie said.

"And why would we do that?"

"To catch him, of course. Don't you want to know who it is?"

"Sure," I said, turning toward her. "But I don't want to die finding out. We'll wait for him to leave and dig up the body. I can snap pictures with my phone. That'll convince your uncle I'm telling the truth."

Covering the grave took less time than digging it. The stranger stomped down the dirt and then, rather than going back to his horse as I'd expected, he wandered to the edge of the cemetery. With his spade he scooped up large clumps of grass and carefully placed the sod over the grave. Dousing the light, he strolled to his horse and hooked the lantern over the saddle horn.

Stars blazed bright against the blackness. Gaslit street-lights from Deadwood's Main Street provided an amber hue against the black hills. The mysterious stranger stood with his back to us, his silhouette framed against the night sky. I half expected him to light a cigarette and blow smoke rings, pull out a harmonica, and play a melancholy cowboy tune. Instead, he placed his hands on his hips and arched his back, stretching.

After a few seconds I realized I'd stopped breathing. So had Annie. The sight of him so close and obviously armed with a revolver had turned us into statues.

At last he gathered the reins and walked his horse under the archway and back toward the trail, his head bobbing side-to-side until he disappeared.

I exhaled.

"How long do we wait?"

I hesitated before answering Annie. I wanted to make certain the man was gone.

"A while," I replied.

"You planning to dig up that body with your hands?"

"If I have to, yes."

"Wouldn't it be easier if we just went back and told Uncle Walt?"

"Told him what? That there's a body buried in Boot Hill? Isn't that sort of the point of a graveyard? All I need is a picture of the face. That should be enough to convince your uncle I'm not crazy."

"Nick?"

"He still might not believe me though. Might think I staged it."

"Nick!"

"For all I know that could be your uncle we just saw. Which means if I show him the pictures he's going to know—"

"Nick, I think there's someone…"

I caught movement out of the corner of my eye, pivoted, and leapt backwards, tumbling into Annie. If I'd jumped a half second later the shovel would have split my skull. The blade whooshed past and clanked against the rocks. I rolled onto my elbow and tried to stand but my attacker pounced, grabbing my jacket and bouncing my head off shale so hard that it felt like he was trying to crack a walnut.

He'd come at us from my right and slightly behind, slipping through a narrow slot where the base of the cliff joined the rocks. Somehow he'd remained below the brow of the graveyard and crept back and around, apparently moving very quickly.

He raised his fist to pound my face. As he did, I bucked and swung my legs, clipping him behind and just above his ankles. He fell hard, releasing a loud "harrumph." Annie yanked away the bandana, gasped, and grabbed my hand, pulling me away just as the killer lunged for my collar. We made no effort to keep quiet, sprinting back across the weeds, jumping over headstones and the iron fence. We went skidding and tripping down the trail, bouncing off a cactus and a bush and making a horrible racket.

When we reached the dry creek bed, I followed Annie down the gully, coming out on a service road. Her horse stood in the small cluster of pines just where we'd left it.

"Ride back to town and don't stop until you reach the stables," she said, thrusting the reins into my hands. "Put her in the corral. I'll come by later and bed her down."

"Come on, we'll both ride her. The two of us don't weigh that much."

"She's nursing a sore tendon, and I don't want to chance it," Annie countered. "I'll follow this road and walk back to town. Hurry, before he catches you." Before I could stop her, she fed my foot into the stirrup, adding, "Try not to fall off. If I'm lucky, he'll see you riding away and follow. Now go!"

"But what about the marshal? We have to tell him what we saw."

"My uncle can't know about this."

"What? Why?"

"Not a word. Not to anyone."

"But I have to tell the marshal."

"Especially not him. I'll find you in the morning and explain everything. Now ride!"

CHAPTER SIX
NOT A GHOST OF A CHANCE

Rain pelted the tin roof, its thunderous drumming prompting me to burrow beneath the covers as I chased the fragments of my fleeting vision. In my dream I rode a grizzly the size of a buffalo. The saddle kept sliding sideways, and no matter how hard I tried, I couldn't keep my bare feet in the stirrups. Each time the beast reared onto its hind legs, the saddle shifted a little further, threatening to dump me. I was certain as soon as I fell, the bear would pounce, ripping me to pieces.

In my dream I gripped the reins and shifted my weight, swaying side-to-side as the lumbering beast foraged through the forest, snarling and snapping, its paws leaving huge craters in the soft dirt. Every few feet the grizzly would twist its head, eyeing me with dead, chestnut eyes. The yellow bandana tied across its snout had slid down, exposing its long fangs dripping with saliva.

In my dream, beyond a mossy meadow stood a blacksmith shop. A single jaundiced ray of light peeked out from the small window. Annie stood on the tiny front porch, waving as if welcoming me home from a long journey. I wanted to slow the bear but didn't know how; I only knew that once the bear caught her scent he'd charge and rip her apart. I screamed to God, begging him to help.

Annie stepped off the porch and walked toward us as if she couldn't see the beast under me. The bear's thunderous growling ricocheted off the canopy of trees, drowning out my frantic pleadings. As the bear lunged for her throat I saw that she was blind. Two silver coins covered her eye sockets. The bear collided with Annie, tumbling and rolling until I found myself buried under the weight of the grizzly's scratchy pelt.

I bolted upright in bed and kicked off the heavy blanket. The sound of rain pounded the roof, blasting away the last fragments of my nightmare.

Thunder rumbled. I swung my feet over the side and rocked forward, rubbing sleep from my eyes. Fat raindrops pelted the windowpanes, blurring the pewter dawn sky. I hit the bathroom, dressed, and walked onto the porch, pulling a rocker away from the railing. Rain cascaded off the metal roof, creating a transparent curtain of silver. Through the rain I gazed up the road toward the corral and blacksmith shop.

No bear. No mutilated Annie. Nothing but a cratered land-scape of moist red earth and copper puddles.

The dream bothered me. Not because of the bear. I'd become accustomed to those kinds of nightmares. You study enough photographs of crime scenes and corpses and the grue-some images morph into a collage of graphic dreams. It was my praying that left me unsettled. I didn't—pray, that is. And yet in my dream I'd begged God to get me off the bear and Annie back inside the blacksmith shop where she would be safe.

I sat on the porch, thinking about my midnight encoun-ter and how close I'd come to having my skull caved in by a shovel. I also wondered about Annie. I had kept my word. I'd returned the horse to the O.K. Corral as instructed and snuck back into my room. But now I had to decide: keep quiet as Annie had asked or break my promise and tell Buckleberry that Billy the Kid's body was buried in Boot Hill. I thought about how frightened Annie had looked when we'd split up. Why had she been so insistent that I not say a word—not even to the marshal?

Was he the one she'd seen? And if so, if he killed Billy, why tell Annie to keep an eye on me? It didn't make sense. I thought back to the note I'd found in the stagecoach. Given how they'd parked the stagecoach beside the barn, any one of five people had access to my knapsack—Mom, Dad, Wendy, Buckleberry, and his deputy. No, six. The driver of the Char-ger. Seven if you counted Annie. She could've been skulking about without any of us knowing it.

One thing was certain. I had too many unanswered ques-tions, and only Annie knew the real identity of the killer—and it terrified her.

A fence of fog formed along the creek, separating our bunk-house from the main drive leading into town.

"You're up early." My sister stepped from her room cocooned in a blanket.

"Rain woke me. You?"

"Dad's snoring."

Our parents' suite separated my closet-sized room from Wendy's. Given the way she'd bragged earlier about the fire-place, I gathered my sister's room had features mine lacked. Features like a shower that worked and a toilet that didn't run constantly.

Wendy settled into the rocker beside me. "Wonder if they'll still have the buffalo hunt."

I glanced over and surveyed the sky. At the base of the mountain range, clouds dangled thin streamers of rain. "You remember yesterday when I was giving you a hard time about believing in ghosts?"

"I didn't exactly say I believed in them. I just find them interesting is all."

"Sit still. I want to read you something."

I quietly opened the screen door to my room, stepped in, and returned with a red fake-leather book.

"Where'd you get that?" she asked, eyeing the Gideon Bible.

"In my dresser when I checked it. Weird thing is, someone has marked it up. Here, let me show you."

I opened the book to the dog-eared pages and read Wendy the sections marked with a yellow highlighter. The verses mentioned ghosts and dead people communicating with witches and mummies staggering out from tombs.

"It's like someone *wanted* me to find this, you know?"

"Or maybe they just forgot to take their Bible home with them."

"It's a complimentary copy. See?" I pointed to the gold embossing on the back cover advertising Campfire Cowboy Ministries and their web address. I asked Wendy, "Is there one in your room?"

Wendy shook her head. "I got a basket of candy, fruit, and nuts. Oh, and a small poetry book that I just love."

"Listen to this." I opened the Bible to one of the marked pages. "*The bodies of many holy people who had died were raised to life. They came out of the tombs after Jesus's resurrection and went into the holy city and appeared to many people.*"

"So?"

"Don't you see? It's like *Night of the Living Dead*. There's a whole section in here about people becoming vampires."

"Really? Show me!"

Wendy leaned over and I pointed to a section talking about a group of guys eating flesh and drinking blood.

I said, "Maybe this ghost nonsense isn't so far-fetched after all."

Mom peeked out and warned us to keep it down, that Dad was still sleeping.

"Hey, Mom, you're not going to believe what Nick just told me. Now he thinks there *are* such things as ghosts."

"I didn't say that."

Mom stepped onto the porch and gently closed the screen door. Noticing the small red Bible she said, "I don't know that I would necessarily believe everything you read in *that* book.

Back then people knew a lot less about science and how the world worked. It's been my experience that if you try to have a reasonable debate with someone who takes the Bible literally, they end up calling you an overeducated elitist who doesn't believe in God."

"Wow, Mom. I've never heard you talk about anyone like that."

"Please understand, son. It's not what's *in* the Bible that bothers me. It's what it does to people. They just seem to lose the ability to reason and think for themselves. But if I'd known coming here would have raised these sorts of questions, I'd have voted for Las Vegas."

"I'm glad we didn't. I'm having a blast now that there's a murder to solve."

"He means a gun blast," Wendy said.

Mom peeped over her shoulder, then back at us. "Dad's up. Guess I better hop in the shower before he uses all the hot water." Mom turned to go inside and added, "You know, Nick, there's no way to prove that what's in the Bible is true or not."

"I know, Mom."

"Or that there is a God. What I'm saying is, you can gather all the clues you want, but in the end, it's just a matter of believing something you can't prove. I would think you of all people would have trouble with that."

Mom returned to her room. Wendy followed, leaving me alone on the porch to make sense of the bizarre Bible verses.

As I thought back to my nightmare, an oppressive dread settled over me. I remembered it had started with me in the barn near where I'd seen the Dodge Charger. The stall doors were open. Fresh sawdust covered the floor, emitting a sweet, woody smell. I'd been standing there burrowing my bare toes in the sawdust when I felt something sticky on the balls of my feet. When I lifted my leg I saw I'd been standing in a puddle of blood. I followed the trail into an empty stall. Annie's horse lay on its side, a large gash in its left hindquarter. Next to the animal was a worm-eaten sign, similar to the one we'd seen at the base of Boot Hill, except instead of faded painted letters, someone had drawn a smiley face in blood—a crude circle with two beady eyes and a crooked smile. Beneath the sign and next to the horse lay Annie's sombrero. There was a single bullet hole through the front. I knew better than to look under it—I knew what I'd find when I did. I peeked anyway. Annie's silver-coin eyes peered up at me, her face pale, lips gray. In her mouth were the keys to the Charger.

I gazed across the silver puddles toward the O.K. Corral with a brooding sense of dread. Whoever it was that we'd seen in the graveyard had followed me home. They had waited in the darkness and invaded my dreams, chasing away the bravado I'd felt the evening before when the marshal had deputized me.

Question was, were they still following me, or was a phantom killer stalking me?

CHAPTER SEVEN
THINGS NOT OKAY AT THE O.K. CORRAL

Things were *not* okay at the O.K. Corral. For one, my eyewitness to the graveyard attack on Boot Hill was late. For another, the rain had temporarily washed out our buffalo hunt. Fine by me—I'd have more time to talk to Annie. Only problem was, after checking the stalls, blacksmith shop, and tack room, the only people I found were grumbling guests arguing about whether we should attend a cowboy poetry reading in the tanner's shop or take a ride on the Big Sky train. While the crowd bickered, I wandered up the drive to the guardhouse to chat with the security guard.

"Well now let me see," said Wyatt Earp, making room for me in his small guardhouse. "Yesterday afternoon. At my age, it's hard to remember back that far."

He sat in a wooden swivel chair wearing a tawny leather vest, green shirt faded to the color of okra, and black jeans. He'd hooked a pair of Tony Lama boots on the edge of his tiny desk and locked his hands behind his downy white head while he gazed up at the ceiling.

"Stepped away to reset the security system 'bout the time you folks pulled up. That's why I wasn't here when you arrived."

He rubbed his forehead with the pad of his thumb as if trying to conjure up a memory. The cramped room smelled of burned coffee. A bow-hunting magazine lay open on his small desk.

"A coyote must've jumped the fence and set it off," Earp continued, pointing to the flashing green light on the security panel. "I couldn't have been gone more than fifteen minutes."

"You sure? No chance you were gone longer?"

"Oh sure. Anything's possible. But the marshal, he gets upset if he calls up here and no one answers. That time of the day I wasn't too worried. Weren't expecting but the one vehicle—yours. And your mom had called to say you were running late. Good thing she phoned too. I'd 'bout decided to lock up for the evening and walk down for dinner."

I glanced at his empty holster. This was the thing I remembered from our arrival; how when he'd dismounted and approached our car I'd thought it odd that a security guard would be wearing a holster but not a gun.

"Where's your sidearm?"

"Loaned it to Jess. Called yesterday afternoon asking if he could borrow mine. Told me to leave it on a nail in the first stall of the barn. He'd pick it up there."

"Did he say why?"

"Misplaced his. Not the first time it's happened. Jess tends to forget things. Not that I have any room to talk. Anyhow, I knew he'd need it for that scene in the saloon last night. Hard to gun down that hayseed farmer without a piece."

"Except that it wasn't loaded," I replied. This make-believe gunfight business was definitely getting on my nerves.

"You're right there," Earp said. "Mine never is anyway. Not with anything but blanks. Doesn't mean it can't shoot real bullets though. But I don't have a permit to carry a loaded sidearm. Got a hunting license but that's for shooting coyotes and prairie dogs and such. Fact is, no one in Deadwood carries a loaded weapon but the marshal and his deputy. They're the only real sworn peace officers. The rest of us just have these for show."

"So you left your gun in Lazy Jack's at what time?"

Wyatt Earp swirled his coffee and frowned. "Let's see. You folks got here a little before six. Jess called maybe a couple hours earlier. If I had to make a guess, I'd say I walked down to the barn and dropped it off around four thirty. Maybe a tad earlier."

"Was there anyone with you while you reset the alarm?" This was the question I'd been waiting to ask. If someone could verify his story, my list of suspects became smaller, though I doubted Wyatt Earp was the killer. He was definitely rounder and shorter than the man I'd seen in the graveyard.

He shook his head. "Never is. We run a thin staff here. Didn't used to be that way. Few years back I had an assistant, but not anymore."

"So no one can verify where you were just before we arrived?"

A smile creased Wyatt's lips. "Reckon not. 'Course if you're thinkin' I was at Lazy Jack's right 'fore you pulled up, then my Marge would have to be some kind of fast racehorse. See, for me to ride from here to that barn and shoot someone, then get to the place where the fence needed fixing and back 'fore you folks arrived would take close to forty-five minutes. And that wouldn't even hardly give me time to hop off and restring the wire in that busted section."

"So if I look at that fence I'll find where you made the repair?"

"Take you there myself if you like. Course you'll need a ride. Marge can't carry the two of us. Can barely carry me. You can get yourself a horse and ride down there yourself. Have to have one of the hands go with you, though. Not supposed to let guests ride alone. 'Cept for if they're ridin' a pony. Fall off a pony and we'd probably sue you for clumsiness."

He smiled at his lame joke; I did not.

"That's how come they make you sign those waivers. Bust a bone, it's on you. Here, I'll show you where the break was."

Wyatt pulled a welcome map from the display case and circled a spot near a green area marked "nature preserve."

"What you do is, ride back up this road about a quarter mile. You'll come to a steer skull. The pair of horns points east. Head off that way and when you come to the ditch, follow it a quarter mile until you see a watering hole. Then turn south. You'll see where the fence starts. When you get to a wide patch of sagebrush, you'll find the new section. Shiny as a new nickel that wire is." Wyatt blew steam from his cup and sipped. "If you want to, we'll ride out there now and take a look."

"Maybe later." He still had the same jolly smile, but I had a feeling my questions had put him on edge somewhat. "Who would benefit from Billy the Kid's death?"

Earp shifted in his chair and looked out the window. "Been wondering when you'd get to that one. Given it some thought too. Can't think of a soul unless it's Jess. I know, sounds bad me saying that. What with what I just told you 'bout my gun and all. But the two of them were up for the supporting role in the remake of *Rio Bravo*."

"So it's possible your gun *is* the murder weapon?"

"Hold on, partner. Didn't say that. You asked me who stands to gain if something happened to Billy. I'm saying the two of them were both angling for the same role. Don't mean Jess had anything to do with Bill's death—assuming Bill *is* dead. Which I doubt. Takes a special kind of man to shoot someone. Least that's what I hear."

"Is the actor who plays Jesse James that kind of someone?"

"Jess? Don't rightly know. Could be. He can be hotheaded sometimes. Got a reputation as a brawler. Been questioned about it a few times too. Involved in a few scuffles in bars. Last one led to an assault charge. Not sure how that turned out. But that don't make him a murderer."

"Have you asked him about your gun?"

"Didn't see any reason to. You're the only one who's taken an interest in it. And like I said earlier, I only wear it for decoration. I figured Jess would return it once he found his. But eventually I will need it back. Lose that revolver and it comes out of my paycheck. One like that, a replica of a .44 caliber Smith & Wesson Schofield would set me back a good piece of change."

Wyatt folded his arms across his chest and studied me. I wondered if in another setting, like maybe in a hayloft with a grudge, he would be as friendly.

"You seem pretty certain Billy was killed," said Earp. "You got any evidence to prove it? I mean, other than what you *think* you saw in the barn?"

The good ones are like that, feigning ignorance, stumbling over their story. They drop in facts here and there that the investigator probably already knows. When they see which way the questioning is going, they send the detective down a rabbit trail, feeding him bits of information that have no bearing on the case. Wyatt Earp seemed like the white rabbit from Alice in Wonderland white rabbit, wiggling a white tail at me and watching to see if I'd follow.

"I get lots of practice putting pieces together," I said at last. "I don't always guess right, but I do more times than not."

"But you don't really have any evidence," said Wyatt, erasing that grandfatherly smile. "I mean, fact is you're just *playing* detective, aren't you? This isn't like a *real* crime in a *real* town where you could *really* get hurt if you got too close to the truth."

I couldn't tell if his words were a threat or a warning. Wyatt Earp didn't strike me as a cold-blooded killer, but if I'd learned anything from studying true crime case files, it was that even the most seasoned law officer could become a killer.

"No, I've never actually been in the room with a murderer," I said.

"Don't look so disappointed, partner. Who knows, maybe one day you'll get the chance."

I pulled on my jacket. "I better get back to the corral before Mom and Dad wonder what happened to me."

Earp asked, "Buffalo roundup still on?"

"Too wet. They're talking about either doing the train ride or the cowboy poetry reading."

"Shame. A lot of folks say the buffalo hunt is the best part of their vacation. Takes you right by the Native American burial grounds. 'Course the train does too, but it doesn't stop. You know they say it's haunted, right?"

"The train?" I asked.

"Native American mounds. People swear they've seen campfires snuffed out, trees rustling even when there's no wind, animals acting strange. Hard to know what goes on up there once that phantom fog rolls in. Covers the ground every place 'cept over the grave mounds themselves. Now, if you really want to investigate spooks and such, that's where I'd be spending my time."

I thanked Wyatt Earp, exited the guardhouse, and walked back toward the O.K. Corral. As I passed Tex's Tannery Depot, I pictured the old man in his comfy little security booth with his Tony Lama leather boots propped up on the desk, cup of coffee in his hand, and smug smile at having sent that "young whippersnapper detective" down a bunny trail.

The train whistle blew. Mom, Dad, and Wendy had already boarded while I had interviewed Earp. I jogged toward the train station, reaching the loading platform just as the last guest boarded the Big Sky. I stepped aboard and snagged a seat in the last row of the passenger car next to the window. Moments later the train lurched and pulled away from the station, ushering in the start of the great Reading Railroad train ride. Near the front of the car a rawhide-tough cowboy rose from his seat, opened a small hardback book, and began reading a ballad by poet Donn Taylor. Wendy squealed with delight. I groaned.

Compromise is a killer, and the best way to ruin a good time is to include someone like me who has no appreciation for sonnets, bonnets, and prairie-home prose. But, as I was about to discover, there are worse things than being trapped on a train with a poetry-reading cowboy.

CHAPTER EIGHT
ROUGHING IT ON THE READING RAILROAD

The Big Sky rambled along over hill and dale as the train's tracks traced the curves and dips of a winding creek. Outside my window, elk grazed in misty meadows and prairie dogs scurried across grassy fields before disappearing into their burrows. Inside, I thought of Annie.

The business in the graveyard at Boot Hill left me rattled, and it wasn't just that I'd almost had my skull caved in by a shovel. That was scary enough, but the way Annie reacted when we reached her horse and then the dream ... Was my grizzly nightmare a premonition? A warning of trouble to come? Or was it (like Mom was always telling me) the result of downing junk food just before bedtime? I couldn't imagine that a fistful of M&M's and Skittles could ignite such gruesome thoughts, but *something* had tripped my imaginary security fence and awakened me.

Then there was Annie's mysterious absence at the not so O.K. Corral.

On we choo-choo-chugged toward Rattlesnake Gulch and Twilight Tunnel. Gold curtain tassels swayed; steel wheels vibrated beneath my sneakers. Closing my eyes, I immediately thought of Annie. I slouched in my seat and rested my head against the worn leather cushion. I like planes okay. They're fun on takeoff and landings—unless there's ice on the wings and runway, which there is sometimes where we live. But there's something personal about a train. Maybe it's the rocking motion and the constant drone of the locomotive's engine. On a deeper, subconscious level, maybe riding a train takes me back to before I was born and was jostling around in my mother's belly and hearing muffled voices but not caring because I didn't know the dangers that lay just beyond the walls of my protective bubble.

I think about this sort of stuff when I'd rather not think about what's really bothering me, and right then I didn't want to think about Annie and Billy the Kid's killer.

But I did anyway.

My conversation with Wyatt Earp concerned me. His explanation for why he'd been away from his post seemed too convenient. Without an eyewitness to verify his whereabouts during the murder, he could have been anywhere, including the barn. He didn't *look* like a murderer, but I'd studied enough real murders to know cold-blooded killers rarely look dangerous. They're schoolteachers and youth pastors and stay-at-home-moms who flip out under pressure. Wyatt Earp might have been fixing the fence. Or he might have been fixing it so Bill Bell never took another breath. I wouldn't know for certain until I learned more about Earp's needs. Find his motive and I might have the killer.

Then there was Marshal Buckleberry. Even though he'd deputized me, he hadn't shown any real interest in taking the murder seriously. I had the impression that for him, the killing of Billy the Kid and my infatuation with the murder was a joke: some extracurricular activity meant to keep my parents happy and me occupied. What better cover than to say he let a kid detective investigate the crime and found no evidence of a murder?

The door swung open next to me. I peeked out and saw Dad enter the passenger car.

"We missed you this morning at breakfast," he announced, taking the seat beside me. "Everything okay?"

I told him I wasn't interested in sitting around listening to people debate how they were going to spend their vacation, especially since I had a murder to solve.

"So you still think that scene you saw in the hayloft was real and not just two actors practicing?"

"I know it, Dad. No one can stare at the ceiling that long without blinking."

"Okay. Just wanted to make sure our vacation isn't boring you."

"It's a lot more exciting than I expected. Thanks for going to bat for me with the marshal."

"Just keep in mind, Nick. He's doing you a favor. Don't do anything that'll give him or me a reason to regret this."

Mom and Wendy sat in front of Dad and me. Other passengers were still filtering in and getting settled. At the front of the car the conductor pulled out a small leather book and began reading. I slumped against the window, enduring a ballad about a black crow. The track had veered away from the creek and begun a long, curving climb up the mountain. Below my window a muddy river wound its way through a deep gorge. The train's whistle rebounded off canyon walls, giving the experience a nostalgic flavor.

After polite applause, the conductor introduced our next lecturer: a "rip-snorting, hard-charging, straight-shooting cowpoke comic named Quick Draw Guffaw."

I took this as my cue to stretch my legs and wander the train, checking out the dining car (vending machines), gambling car (small booths set up for bingo), and restroom car (Gunslingers, Miss Kitty). Tour completed, I returned to my seat.

"Since many of you are unfamiliar with the ways and history of these parts," Guffaw announced, "I'd like to give a full and inaccurate accounting of the significant historic events that shaped the Old West."

Dad nudged me with his elbow. "You listening, Nick?"

I nodded, even though my mind was still on the case. And on the Bible in my room. I wanted to ask Dad if he and Mom had found a Bible marked up with verses about ghosts but decided against it. I figured the less I said about the scary scripture, the easier it would be for me to determine if they were clues to the killer.

Guffaw, wearing white pants, vest, and coat, stood erect, one hand resting on the doorway for balance, the other clasping an unlit cigar. "Years ago in a galaxy far, far away, during a time when writers such as Mark Twain, John Steinbeck, and Louis L'Amour wrote descriptive and sometimes boring novels about the harsh environment settlers faced on the great American frontier, buffalo roamed and ranged and left large pie-shaped piles, all-natural organic fertilizer, on the messy plains. This made tracking, hunting, and killing buffalo easy. You only needed to follow the smell."

I sat up, smiling. Dad, too.

"Whole states, many of which hadn't even been invented yet, scrambled to accommodate the buffalo; not to mention those notoriously wily varmints, politicians."

Dad leaned over. "Better than the poetry reading?"

"Definitely. And way better than the history lectures I got in civics class."

Wendy turned and glared. "Would you two hush? I can't hear."

"Within this rustic, rustbelt political landscape," Guffaw continued, "young male and female deer and antelope frolicked and fawned all over each other to such a degree that parents often forbade these rambunctious couples from seeing each other outside of school. This led to such great works of literature as *Romeo and Juliet*, from which we get the classic line: 'Romeo, Romeo, where art thou commuter train to Chicago, oh Romeo?'"

I saw the side of Mom's face and her furrowed brow. Leaning forward I explained that the city of Joliet was the fourth largest city in the state of Illinois, located just forty-five miles southwest of Chicago. She brightened once she caught on to the punch line.

"Meanwhile in the Old West, displaced residents from Manhattan's Upper West Side sat around campfires singing folk songs and wearing mink stoles and listening to really bad harmonica music."

The Big Sky turned away from the river and gorge and chugged toward a series of chimney-shaped outcroppings. Goats stood on rocky slopes eyeing the train as it passed. Just for fun I glanced around to see if Annie had snuck aboard without me noticing, but I didn't see her.

"Such was the era of western exploration. A period in American history unlike any before it. And hopefully never to be seen again. This was America's first 'lost generation.' A term normally ascribed to uneducated and unemployable teens, but which fit these hearty folks due to the fact that no one, not even the renowned explorers Huey Lewis and the Dave Clark candy bar, had a clue what they were doing or where they were going since the GPS and highway maps hadn't been invented yet. What am I saying? HIGHWAYS HADN'T BEEN INVENTED. In fact, the 75-watt GE lightbulb was just a flicker in the eye of the American inventor 'Tommy Boy' Edison."

I could tell the comic was feeding off the audience's energy, holding the pause just long enough to draw the listeners forward in their seats. There's a skill to holding a crowd's attention. Last semester we studied the technique in drama class. Not that I was any good at acting or wanted to be in a play.

But the course was an easy A because it focused primarily on technique and if there was one thing I'm good at, it's analyzing facts and memorizing technique. That's one reason all this detective stuff is so much fun for me.

I nudged Dad. "I need to get up and move around."

"But this guy's a hoot. Don't tell me you're bored."

"Oh, no. He's way better than the poetry guy. But I'm tired of sitting."

No further explanation needed. Dad understood, even if Mom didn't.

The one time I'd mentioned to my father how hard it was for me to sit still, he'd shared how when he was a boy he suffered from what Grandmamma Caden called "fidgety pants."

"You probably got it from me, Nick. Not that I'm an expert on ADD or anything. Your mom's the one who keeps up with all these childhood syndromes. But I almost flunked ninth grade because I couldn't stay seated. Teacher kept threatening to tie me into my chair. Part of it was because I was bored and spent too much time daydreaming. Now it's not so bad. Only flares up when I'm sitting in a sales meeting or listening to your sister recite those poems she writes," he'd said, winking.

He swung his legs and I slid out, mirroring the comic cowboy's posture by taking a position at the rear of the car.

"Bushwhackers, desperados, and hornswagglers roamed, ranged, and terrified the settlers of the Old West, ruling the Bad Lands from the Dakotas to Duluth, adding a mystical aura to U.S. social studies classes. Tracking these lawless men was easy. You only needed to follow the smell. The indigenous people—Indians, so named in honor of a country clear on the other side of the globe—found themselves rounded up and shuttled onto tour buses where they spent days, sometimes months, visiting scenic national monuments like the Grand Canyon, Yellowstone National Park, and Frank Stoeber's giant ball of twine in Cawker City, Kansas. As often happens during such tours, the buses broke down, leaving the group stranded in desolate areas. The marooned passengers called such places Death Valley, Broken Bow, and Cleveland. Miles from civilization and out of cell phone range, these resolute Native Americans began walking along a path known as the Trail of Tears—so called because of the scorching hot desert sand and the fact that the very last pair of moccasins in all of the United States was at that very moment in history on the feet of a guy named James Fenimore Gary Cooper, a famous American author who would later write a poem that would become mandatory reading in all U.S. literature classes, but at the time was struggling to find a publisher due to Cooper's insistence that the title remain, *The Last of the Moccasins.*"

The train's side-to-side rocking lessened, and I noticed we'd begun to slow. Holding onto the back of Dad's seat, I leaned toward the window and peered out. A hand-lettered sign warned that we'd reached HOLE IN THE WALL JUNCTION: HOME TO BROWN BARES (*Not another misspelling.*) AND BLACK BART. The shudder of steel wheels braking brought the Big Sky to a halt, and steam billowed outside our windows. Quick Draw Guffaw announced that we'd reached the halfway point of our ride and he would be taking a break while the engine took on water. Passengers were free to disembark and have their picture taken with him in front of the locomotive.

I filed out with the others and found myself standing near the base of an old mining camp. Rusty picks, sifting pans, and wooden flues lay scattered about the ground. A rocky stream sliced through the camp and disappeared into a gully choked with scrub trees and sagebrush. Sheer rock walls towered above the russet peaks. Fractured clouds left wide patches of blue poking through gray. While others lined up to have their pictures taken in front of the cowcatcher, I headed in the opposite direction and caught not a cow, but a break in the case.

Annie rode toward us on her black mare. Had it not been for her reddish-blonde ponytail bouncing off her shoulders I might have mistaken her for Black Bart, with her black hat sitting snugly on her head, front brim flattened by wind and speed, black pants, shirt, and leather vest.

I stood in the middle of the tracks behind the caboose, arms folded across my chest, head slightly cocked, giving her my best John Wayne, Clint Eastwood, Val Kilmer stance. I hoped to appear indifferent, but honestly I was relieved. I feared something had happened to her.

Tugging on the reins, she brought her horse to a stop and dismounted.

"Oversleep?" I said dryly.

"Needed to take care of some things."

"You could've left a message with someone at the corral. I waited a long time."

"I said I was busy, okay? You're not my mom, you know."

Taking the reins, she walked her horse up the tracks and let it drink from the rocky stream.

"Just saying, meeting at the corral was your idea, not mine."

She pushed the hat back on her head and wiped her brow with the back of her riding glove. When she did, I noticed the saffron bruise just below her hairline.

I stepped toward her to get a better look. "Did you get walloped?"

"Did I get what?"

"Looks like you ran into a tree," I said, rubbing my thumb over the contusion. "Or a fist."

"I … fell off my horse."

She pushed my hand away and ruffled her bangs.

Leaning closer I replied, "Face first and on your head?"

"Hey, look. It's not like you're an expert on horseback riding, okay? The buckle on my saddle broke and I slipped off. End of story."

"Sure, whatever. So who was it, really?"

She stared upwards with a look of surprise. "I told you! Nobody. I fell."

"I meant, who did we see last night in the graveyard. You said you'd tell me."

"I, ah … was mistaken."

"Oh, come on. You know exactly who it was."

"Boy, my uncle is right. You *are* paranoid."

"Here's what I know. Someone took a swing at me with a shovel."

"We were trespassing. You read the sign."

It was obvious she was covering for somebody. Who, I couldn't tell. But pushing her for answers wasn't going to get me the name of the killer. *Better to play along and let the truth find me.*

"So no one threatened you?" I said. "No one told you to keep quiet about what you saw?"

She shook her head. "The only reason I rode out here was to tell you to be careful." Leaning into me, she murmured, "And to maybe not ask so many questions. This isn't a game, Nick."

"So that means it's okay if I go to the marshal and tell him what we saw?"

"I'd rather you didn't."

"But you just said—"

I hadn't realized she'd been resting her hand on my hip until she pulled away. "Couldn't we just keep it our little secret for now?"

"But Billy the Kid's body is buried up there."

"Please, Nick. If you tell my uncle about what we saw he'll want to know why I was hanging out with you after midnight. He's very protective. Still treats me like I'm in grade school. Deal?"

"For now," I answered. "But at some point I'll have to tell him about the body buried on Boot Hill."

"Later is fine. Just not now."

CHAPTER NINE
THE DALTON GANG

The train's shrill whistle blast hustled us back aboard the Big Sky. Annie climbed aboard her horse and galloped away. I returned to my seat in the passenger car. Minutes later we rolled away from the Hole in the Wall Junction, and the comic cowboy returned to his act.

"After many months of walking on the Trail of Tears, the Native Americans finally reached their destination—Detroit. Having failed again to find a peaceful place void of riots, gangs, and interstates choked with American-made automobiles, the Native Americans moved west and settled in the desert. Overnight, a new industry blossomed in the middle of this barren wasteland—gambling."

"Soon casinos competed with sagebrush on the forlorn moonscape, a countryside so void of moisture that the Native Americans aptly named it Loss Vegas. The name stuck and soon the more industrious tribal members subdivided the sandlots into city blocks, choking it with strip malls and cheap hotels that rented rooms by the hour. Unaccustomed to running such sprawling and corrupt institutions, the Native Americans turned the management of these casinos, nightclubs, and brothels over to government officials who, in turn, outsourced the work to another tribe of indigenous people. A tribe hunkered on the shores of New Jersey who had spent years beating plowshares into swords and knee-caps into pulp. This tribe was known simply as "The Mob." Soon, crowds flocked to the desert oasis to listen to really old and inebriated singers mumble songs no one had ever heard of. The Wild West had been tamed. And so it remains tame to this day. Only ... not all the Wild West is tamed, and if you'll look out the windows to your right, you'll see what I mean."

Pulling alongside the train was a posse of riders kicking up a cloud of dust.

Bursting into the car, the conductor shrieked: "The Dalton Gang!"

Aiming pistols into the air and firing at random, the Daltons pressed closer to the train. Out my window I saw the lead rider leap from his horse and grab the railing on the steps, swinging himself aboard.

The rest of the gang rode alongside, firing randomly at the train. The window next to me shattered and I ducked. Even though I knew the robbery was staged and the hole where the bullet supposedly hit was planted with some type of small explosive, the bang still left me jumpy. Besides, I couldn't be certain they weren't using real ammo. *Annie did ride all the way out here to warn me to be careful. Was the killer one of the Daltons?*

The train's engineer threw the brake and we lurched forward. The sound of hissing steam blended with the rumble of a boxcar door being rolled open. More gunfire erupted outside my window. Beside me the rear door flew open and in burst a hook-nosed fellow with whiskered cheeks, thick black eyebrows, and a red bandana synched over his mouth and chin. Holding his gun upwards, he fired two shots and ordered us out. I noticed there were no holes in the wood paneling on the ceiling above his head, suggesting to me that his pistol was loaded with blanks. Still, the quick succession of loud bangs produced more shrieks of panic, my sister's sounding the loudest.

Thirty or so passengers filed past my seat. I joined the end of the line, jostled by the comic cowboy bumping into me and urging me to hurry. Outside we lined up beside the train. The gunmen leveled their pistols at us, daring us to move. An older fellow with a rubbery belly sagging over his belt ordered two members of the gang inside the boxcar.

"Big Daddy Dalton," Wendy said to me in a low voice. "I read about him in my welcome packet."

Seconds later there was a small explosion from inside the boxcar. I leaned out and looked down the line far enough to spy a small safe standing near the door of the boxcar.

A sturdy-looking wooden chest flew out and landed on the ground. Big Daddy quickly drew his revolver and fired, blowing off the lock. The two outlaws jumped down from the boxcar and lifted the lid. Inside were bricks of cash, each brick banded with a cord of string. The pair began tossing packets of cash to the other train robbers.

I eyed each member of the gang as they caught the packets of money, trying my best to see if any of their eyes matched those of the man who'd come at me with the shovel.

Daddy Dalton, sitting high in the saddle, slowly walked his horse past us, examining each passenger carefully. We stood with our backs to the railcar, no one speaking. I couldn't be sure, but it sounded like Wendy was sobbing. *Come on, sis. You can't really be scared. It's all an act. Just a Hollywood stunt.*

Daddy Dalton's gaze settled on me; the hair on my neck stiffened.

No, you're not the one I saw on Boot Hill. But that doesn't mean you didn't kill Billy the Kid.

Breaking eye contact, Daddy Dalton called in a mocking voice, "Bushwhackers, desperados, and hornswagglers roamed, ranged, and terrified the settlers of the Old West." Big Daddy aimed his beady eyes at the comic cowboy. "Tracking these lawless men was easy. You only needed to follow the smell."

Wheeling his horse around, Daddy Dalton aimed both revolvers at the comic and fired both guns. The cowboy comic twisted, staggered back. Blood (or corn syrup mixed with red food coloring) soaked his white jacket and vest. In typical dramatic fashion, the comic tried to claw his way up the steps—as though climbing to safety with five bullet holes in his chest and belly would save him. In real life you don't walk, crawl, or stagger away from multiple gunshot wounds. That only works in television.

In real life the body goes into shock, focusing all resources on the injury. It's a primal reaction: find the source of the bleeding, evaluate the damage, and repair it. Big Daddy Dalton wasn't going to give Quick Draw Guffaw that option. Big Daddy emptied his guns into the cowboy, and Guffaw collapsed onto the platform—his top half lying face down on the steps, his legs tangled beneath him, knees resting on the gravel railbed.

Then, like in the saloon, the dead man vanished.

Big Daddy ordered the Dalton boys to mount up. Yanking the reins of his horse, he scowled at me and rode off, leading his men back down the tracks in the direction from which they'd come.

"Come on, Nick," Dad said, rushing toward the bloody steps. "Let's go see how he disappeared."

But I had another idea. My plan was to confront the comic. I was tired of the smoke and mirrors and theatrical magic that kept the guests entertained and me guessing how Billy the Kid's body had disappeared from Lazy Jack's. I wanted to shake the funny actor by the shoulders and force him to explain how both he and the farmer in the saloon vanished. I needed to know if it was possible for someone to pull off a similar stunt in the hayloft. The comic struck me as just enough of an oddball that he might be willing to share a few of Deadwood's secrets.

While Dad went in search of the trapdoor he was sure he'd find built into the steps, I circled around to the other side of the train, confident I'd find the comic resting from and reflecting upon his performance.

I didn't. What I saw instead chilled me. Nearly three hundred yards away, just visible above the bushy tops of a grove of scrub trees, I spied a series of low mounds cloaked in a silver mist. Wispy tendrils of vapor coiled upwards, swirling and swaying like dead spirits dancing.

The Native American burial grounds. Right where Wyatt Earp said they would be. And someone—no, something—is waving to me. Cowboy comic? Dead farmer? Billy the Kid?

The train whistle blew. The conductor ordered us back to our seats.

"Come on, Nick!" Mom yelled out the window to me.

The train started to move. Jogging toward the caboose, I swung myself up and stood watching as the wispy figures melted away.

I shoved my hand into my pocket, felt something, and pulled out ... a lead slug.

CHAPTER TEN
A KILLER IDEA

I sat on my seat examining the slug. *Who dropped this in my pocket? Guffaw when he bumped me from behind exiting the train? Annie snuggling up to me? A ghost?* I shoved the slug back into my pocket, deciding to keep it a secret for now.

As soon as the Big Sky reached the station, I bounded down the steps and went in search of James. If what the old security guard said was true, James might have a motive for killing the young actor, Bill Bell.

I found James sitting on a fence rail chewing on a strand of straw. Red and white checkerboard shirt, brown leather cowboy chaps over blue dungarees. Cowboy hat tipped forward, shielding dark eyes from the high-noon glare. In the circular corral behind James, a rodeo clown bobbed and weaved away from a very large Brahma bull. I approached James, but before I could say a word, he hopped down, gave me a firm handshake, and whacked me on the back like we were best buds.

"Heard you might want to talk to me. Caden, was it? The boy-wonder detective?"

Up close his sun-browned face showed his youth. Black hair lay matted against his forehead. Late teens, early twenties.

He released my hand but maintained his smile. "Marshal said you might have some questions for me. So how can I help you, Deputy?"

I said, "You can start by dropping the act."

"Act?"

"I could ask you where you were last night around midnight, but let's save that for later. First, I want to know if you hit Annie."

"I'm not following you, partner."

I explained how I'd found the marshal's niece visibly shaken earlier that morning and how, when pressed about the incident, she refused to elaborate.

"I don't rightly know how to respond to that," James said. "I've been here all morning breaking these mustangs. Or I should say, they've been breaking me. Haven't seen Annie since last night in the saloon and only then for a moment. Is this about Bill?"

Trying to appear taller, I squared my shoulders and stopped slouching. "I understand you two weren't on the best of terms."

"I didn't hear a question in that."

"Did you and Billy get along?"

"*Do* get along. Yeah, sure. We get along. At least I think so. Why, you hear differently?"

"But weren't you both auditioning for the same movie?"

"You're making that sound a lot more interesting than it was. I was disappointed I didn't get the part, sure. Bill's a good actor. We both took a shot, and he won. Happy for him. 'Sides, he knows all the right people out there. Me? I'm just a struggling actor working on his craft and hoping to catch a break. Getting that part would have been huge but there'll be other roles."

"But with him out of the way, they might take a second look at you, right?"

"Out of the way? You lost me."

"I mean dead."

"Oh, right. 'Cause as far as you're concerned that's what he is. Fact is, Bill's in L.A. 'Least that's what I hear."

"So you deny killing him?"

"You know, for a boy trying to get answers from people you sure have a way of getting on their bad side. Anyway, to answer your question, no, I didn't kill anybody." Raising an eyebrow, he added, "Least, not yet."

"So, there was nothing to this movie competition with Bill Bell then?"

"Look, I never had a real shot at that part in *Rio Bravo*, okay? It was Bill's all the way. He goes to all the right parties and knows the producers by first name. Me? I'd rather let my acting get me the work. And for the most part it does. But if you're asking if I'd do anything to hurt Bill's chances of getting that part, the answer is no. We're friends and competitors, that's it."

"What about the assault charge?"

"See? There you go shooting off the hip and missing everything. That charge you're referring to got tossed. Knew it would be. Nothing but a disagreement with a hothead at a bar who was so drunk he could hardly stand up. He took a swing at me, missed, and hit his head while falling. The proceedings lasted all of twenty minutes. Got any more questions, Deputy Caden?"

The way he said my name made it sound like he was spitting a gulp of sour milk from his mouth.

With less conviction I replied, "Besides you, who else would benefit from Billy's death?"

"See? Now that's a question. Can't think of a soul except the marshal. Bill loaned him fifty grand to keep this tourist trap alive. As I understand it, Bill got in a bind and demanded the marshal start paying him back, but Buckleberry doesn't have it. Probably never will. Shouldn't be telling you this, but the honest truth is this could be our last season at Deadwood. That's why Bill was so anxious to land that movie role. Gets him out of this dead-end town and into the bright lights of Hollywood."

"And you?"

James shrugged. "I'm a survivor. If this place folds, I'll find work."

He adjusted his hat and thumped me on the arm the way a high school quarterback might when he's trying to be friendly with a lower classman.

"Look, Caden. I know this little investigation of yours is a big deal. And I feel bad that your family hauled you all the way out to this place. If I was your age I'd be bored out of my gourd, too. But the fact is, no one was murdered. You were there last night in the saloon. You saw how we do things. Nobody really gets shot. It's all one big put-on. As for Annie, I'm not sure what to tell ya. She's a good girl. A little too talkative for my taste, but I can't imagine why anyone would want to hurt her. Certainly wouldn't be me. Not with her being the marshal's niece. I think what you have here is a lot of loose pieces that you're trying to shoehorn into place."

"If I locate the murder weapon, any chance I'll find your prints on it? Any chance at all?" I watched to see his reaction. But instead of flashing a hint of anger like I'd expected, he laughed—which only made *me* mad.

"Tell ya what, Caden. Snoop around all you want, but odds are you're going to come up dry. Just like the marshal and his big plans for this place. Hang around Deadwood long enough and you'll discover there's nothing here but a whole lot of disappointment."

"You didn't answer the question."

"Call Bill. Ask him how it is with us. He'll tell you the two of us get along just fine. Or ask anyone else in this town. They'll all tell you the same thing. We 'bout done here? I need to get back to them mustangs."

"Almost." I wanted to ask if he was in the graveyard the night before, but I knew he'd deny it even if he was. He certainly *seemed* friendly. But then, so far almost everyone I'd met had been cooperative in their own guarded way.

"Anybody else with you this morning while you were breaking those mustangs?"

He shook his head. "Got here early, just a little before dawn.

I'd probably been working a good half hour before the first hands showed up to get things ready for the guests."

"What type of car do you drive?"

"Wow. That came out of nowhere. Dodge Charger. Why?"

"Where were you yesterday evening between five and six?"

"Well, let's see. Yesterday afternoon I was on my way back from Denver. Left the courthouse a little before noon, grabbed a bite to eat, and drove back. Got here sometime after five. I remember because I had to hurry to get ready for the shootout scene in Sally's."

"And you parked where?"

"In the employee parking lot like always."

"Not in the barn?"

For a moment I saw a fracture in that buddy-buddy facade, but he recovered quickly. "Hey, you know what? You're right. I stopped off at the barn to get something. Just left my car there because it's closer than the lot."

"Wyatt Earp said you called and asked to borrow his gun."

"Oh, I think I see where you're going with this. Sure, I asked to borrow his Schofield, but he must've forgotten. Does that a lot. The old man can barely remember to put in his teeth."

"But you were at Lazy Jack's? For a short while at least?"

"Only long enough to check for Earp's revolver. When I saw it wasn't there, I left. Then a few minutes later, when I dropped off my laundry, I found my piece in a gym bag of dirty socks. How much longer is this going to take? Those mustangs aren't going to break themselves."

"I guess that's it for now. Okay if I stop by later if I have other questions?"

"Sure, Caden. Happy to help."

He gave me a quick smile—just like he'd probably done hundreds of times before when posing for a photo shoot, holding it just long enough for those dark eyes to harden into an icy stare. "Good luck with your investigation, Deputy. Wish I could've been more help."

But he had been. In more ways than he could imagine.

CHAPTER ELEVEN
BANCO DE LOS BANDIDOS

I found James's car parked behind the laundry building in a gravel lot marked IMPLOYEASE ONLY—just like Wyatt Earp said I would. Second row. Two doors over from a mud-splattered pickup tagged with a sheriff's sticker in the back windshield. Given Earp's suggestion that James often let others park his car for him, it made sense I'd find the Charger in the lot. Question was, what happened to Earp's Schofield?

Popping the lock took all of thirty seconds. I'd picked up a rubber wedge, the type used for propping open a door, from the general store and a flat, two-foot long piece of metal from the blacksmith shop. Shoving the wedge between the driver's doorjamb and door, I'd opened a quarter-inch gap just wide enough for the rod. I'd seen this done once when Mom had locked her keys in the car. We'd tried everything to get her car unlocked. Coat hanger slipped through the window, paper clip in the lock. All we ended up doing was scratching the paint.

Thirty minutes after the call, a tow truck driver arrived. He examined the make of the car and returned from his truck with a rubber wedge and long, straight rod. Took him thirty seconds to pop the lock.

The shaft slipped easily through the gap. I tapped the unlock button and heard the lock disengage.

I opened the door, climbed in, and sat in the driver's seat, pulling the door shut. The interior of the bright yellow Charger smelled of leather and sour clothes. I kept looking out the windshield to make sure no one was watching. The last thing I needed was someone accusing me of trying to boost a late-model muscle car.

Fast-food bags, stray fries, and a crumpled parking receipt from a Denver parking garage lay on the passenger's floor mat. I thumbed open the glove box and found a registration card for Dallas Joshua James of Golden, Colorado. Beneath the owner's manual I found a summons for James to appear in court. The date and time matched his account of the previous day. One charge of assault.

I remembered Earp telling me James was a brawler. *Is he the type to hit a young woman? Or gun down a coworker?* I tucked the court summons back in the glove box and felt under the passenger seat.

Sweat erupted on my forehead and I started thinking: *This is no place for a fourteen-year-old to be. No place at all. But I can't go to the marshal with just some crazy story about Billy the Kid being buried on Boot Hill. I need the murder weapon.*

The pounding on the driver's window nearly sent me into orbit. My sister pressed her face against the glass and peered in.

"Whose car is this?" she blurted out.

"None of your business. Now go away."

"Does the marshal know you broke into someone's car? Does Mom know?"

"Wendy, please! I'm working on the case."

"Come on Nick, tell me what you're looking for. I want to help. Is it that dead cowboy's body?"

"No. I found that already."

"You did? Where? Can I see it? Is it gross?"

"I can't tell you where it is but it's not here, okay? Now please go."

"Mom wants you in the saloon right now. We're dressing up like those people on Little House on the Prairie and going to have our picture taken for our Christmas card."

"Tell her I'll be there in a sec."

"She said to come *now.*"

I shut the door and bent over to look under the passenger seat. No gun. I sat up and swept sweat from my face. Wendy marched toward the buildings facing Main Street. I knew she'd tell Mom. She always did when I shut her out like that. But I couldn't risk her blabbing to my parents that I was hunting for a gun. Mom would freak if she knew.

I twisted and felt under the driver's seat. Nothing. I wanted to look in the trunk but didn't dare risk it. Not with employees milling around the rear of the laundry building, smoking. I waited until the lot was empty, then cracked open the door and hit the door lock. Crouching by the side of the car, I snuck to the rear and peeked over the roof. When the last of the workers snuffed out her cigarette and went inside, I walked quickly away from the laundry building toward Sassy Sally's Saloon, wondering where Billy's killer had ditched the murder weapon.

The photographer handed me a sack of clothes and pointed me in the direction of the men's restroom. I peeled off my shirt, shoes, and pants and slipped on the hokey Little House on the Prairie outfit, complete with high-waist pants and suspenders.

"Let's do this," I said, joining my family by the piano.

"Boy, you're bossy," Wendy replied, twirling her parasol over her shoulder. "Especially for someone who kept the rest of us waiting. Did you find what you were looking for?"

I shot her a quick glance and said to the photographer, "Where do you want me to stand?"

The photographer positioned Mom and Dad on either end of the piano. Wendy and I sat on the short bench with our backs to the keys. *How quaint.* I hoped Mom was kidding about the Christmas card idea. I could just imagine what my friends would say if they saw me dressed up like Albert (Albert!—of all names) Ingalls.

Flash. The photographer snapped a series of photos, moved us into different positions, and reeled off a few more shots. He put the camera away and told us the pictures would be up on a flat-panel monitor in just a sec. I told Mom she had my vote.

In the bathroom I changed back into my real clothes and hurried to the marshal's office. Even without a murder weapon, I needed to tell him what I'd seen in the graveyard. Maybe Bill Bell's body would prove to him that I wasn't lying about the murder in the hayloft.

I'd just stepped from the saloon onto Main Street when a bank customer bolted from the bank yelling, "Quick! Get the marshal! The bank's being robbed!" The old woman shuffled away to join the other shopkeepers and townspeople who'd taken cover on the boardwalk and inside stores. A burly man in overalls pulled me behind a porch post and told me to get down. My family cowered inside Sassy Sally's.

"Banco de los Bandidos," Overalls said, lowering his voice. "Muy malo."

Very bad, indeed, I thought, practicing my Spanish.

Seconds later the bandits bolted from the bank. The two men sported drooping mustaches, sombreros, and ponchos. Each carried a bulging gunnysack, which I assumed was full of fake money. From the other end of the street came gunfire. I whirled and saw Marshal Buckleberry coming on at a dead run, firing with both barrels. The taller of the two bandits slung his bag over the horn of the saddle, mounted his horse, and galloped away, yelling, "Yo soy el pan de vida; el que a mí viene, nunca tendrá hambre."

The shorter, rounder bandit struggled to mount his horse. Each time he placed his foot in the stirrup the horse crabbed away, causing the man to hop along in a circle.

The marshal paused and leveled his revolver, ordering the man to drop the money and raise his arms. The bank robber, finally swinging his leg over the saddle, spurred his horse and attempted to gallop away.

Marshal Buckleberry fired two shots, and the rider suddenly plunged backwards, flipped off and over his horse, and landed on his back in a watering trough. The timing and technique were perfect and would have easily won a medal in the Olympics.

A single boot remained visible, its heel hooked on the lip of the watering trough. The crowd cautiously approached, forming a loose horseshoe around the trough. The outlaw remained submerged, eyes wide and round and peering up through clear water. Casually, the marshal bumped the boot off the rim and it sank. Then, just like in the saloon and train, the phantom figure became less defined, as though melting *into* the water. The transformation couldn't have lasted more than two seconds. One moment the bandit was there; the next, poof!

The crowd gasped, then applauded. Mom, Dad, and Wendy clapping the hardest.

I congratulated the marshal on another fine performance and told him I had something to show him. He jerked his head back toward his office at the end of Main Street and told me to wait for him.

The marshal's office shared a feature common to western jails—at least of those jails shown in movies. Two cells stood opposite from each other, separated by a short hallway leading to the rear of the building. The view from just inside the doorway was of a sparse, compact office. Wooden desk, wooden swivel chair. Ring of keys hanging from a peg fastened to a vertical support beam next to one corner of the desk. Above the keys hung an unlit kerosene lantern. On the other side of the support hung a wide leather belt and holster. No gun.

One edge of the beam had been worn smooth, its rough finish almost glossy. I pictured the marshal resting his shoulder against that beam, arms folded across his chest, one boot hooked over the other in a casual pose. Cameras flashing. Hint of a smile frozen on his face. "Come on, boys and girls. Stand over here and get your picture taken with the marshal," he might say, beckoning to the timid.

Like a serpent warming itself on a dusty trail, the marshal had tried to cast himself as nothing more than an easygoing lawman in a make-believe ghost town. A harmless brown stick on the side of a footpath. But I knew better. I'd seen a flash of anger in his eyes when I'd questioned his investigative skills. The challenge from Marshal Buckleberry was clear: bend down and mess with that old brown stick and you'll pay.

I heard the jingle of the marshal's spurs and went in, taking the only spare chair in the room. He moved to the other side of the desk and rolled his chair back, angling it so we could talk over the corner of the desk.

"You let one get away," I told the marshal when he arrived. "Was that part of the act?"

"No act, son. What you saw out there was the real deal." He hung his hat on a peg and pulled the door shut behind him. "I keep telling you this is a ghost town. At some point you'll start believing me."

I explained how I'd done some checking and learned that ghosts and creditors were about the only visitors stopping by Deadwood.

"Sounds like you've been talking to Jess."

"I have."

"He needs to learn to keep his mouth shut. Talking out of character can get you fired."

"Any truth to what he said about you having financial difficulties?"

"He probably made it sound worse than it is. Sour grapes because I didn't give him a glowing endorsement like he wanted. But sure, it's been a tough couple of years. No point acting like it hasn't."

"How bad?"

"This is off the record, you understand. I'm just telling you this because I know you're all wrapped up in this imaginary murder case." He pivoted and pointed out the window toward Main Street. "Bookings are down. Costs keep rising. Insurance has gone through the roof. You have no idea how difficult it can be to run a venture of this size on a shoestring budget. Families don't take trips like they used to. Kids today are into movies and video games. But then I'm not telling you something you don't already know." He leaned back in his chair and propped his feet on his desk. "You said you had something you wanted to show me?"

"I understand you took a loan from Billy the Kid."

"I did?"

"As I understand it, Bill Bell loaned you fifty thousand dollars."

"We're a small county tucked way up in the hills. This town and the tourists it brings are about the only attraction we have in these parts. Except for the ski resorts, of course, but that's seasonal. Good seasonal, but there's a wide spread between May and December, and people need work year-round."

"The economy of Deadwood isn't really my concern, Marshal. But finding Bill Bell's killer is."

The marshal sighed and rocked forward in his chair, looking at me with hound dog eyes.

"Four years ago you wouldn't have recognized this place. We had fresh tar on the highway and plans for a regional airport with shuttle service to Denver. Had a stack of resumes taller than that wastebasket of people wanting to work in Deadwood. Pick of the best actors this side of California. Then the county went and passed a tourism tax. Idea was to get visitors coming to enjoy our county to pay for the road improvements and new school buildings. Sounded like a good idea at the time. First season we hardly noticed the dip in attendance. The next year, bookings were down, but we cut expenses some and did okay. By the next spring I started to notice fewer ads in the chamber of commerce magazine for mom-and-pop shops. You know, the handcrafted quilting boutiques, river tours, eco hikes, those sorts of places. Last summer the price I had been paying for a quarter page ad in the magazine got me the whole back cover. Those ad people did a real nice job. Made us look like Disneyland. Didn't help at all. Ticket sales fell by half. Word had finally gotten around that our county wasn't tourist friendly. That we were milking visitors so every kid in our public schools could have his own tablet. Was a lie, of course, but it's hard to change the public's perception once they get their minds made up."

"You didn't answer my question. Did you and Billy have a

financial agreement of some kind, and if so, was he pressuring you to make good on your end of the arrangement?"

"Bill comes from money. I come from farming and working hard and not much else. Yeah, I'm a little behind on my payments. What of it?"

"Was he pressuring you to pay up?"

"Don't recall that he said one way or the other. Last time I mentioned it to Bill he acted like it wasn't any big deal. You said there was something you wanted to show me?"

I'd planned to mention the incident in the graveyard and see if he'd walk with me up to Boot Hill, but now I couldn't be certain that the marshal wasn't involved somehow. Maybe that's why Annie hadn't wanted to go to her uncle. Maybe he was the one we'd seen on Boot Hill. He was about the same height as the man we'd seen.

I switched tactics and reached into my pocket. Placing the smashed slug on his desk, I said, "Found this earlier today. Any chance you can have it tested?"

"Found it where? In the barn?"

"I'd rather not say."

"That barn's off-limits. You know that, right?"

"Yes, sir. It came from someplace else."

He pulled open a drawer and swept the slug into a small manila envelope. "I have a currier coming by in a few minutes to drop off a few rush supplies for tonight's hoedown. A special barbeque sauce we like in these parts. I'll send it along with the driver."

"Thanks, Marshal." I wasn't sure how to ask my last question so I just blurted out, "Is this Deadwood's last summer?"

The marshal looked away. For a few seconds I thought he

hadn't heard the question. Or had heard and was refusing to answer. Finally, he shifted in his chair and replied, "Doubt it. I can trim the staff a little more. Hate to do it. Most of the ones left started with me. A few volunteered to work part time this year. Only call them when there's a crowd coming. Haven't had to in a long while. Look, you want to talk to Billy and ask him about the loan, be my guest. You heard him on the phone last night. He'll probably be back before you leave."

"I would if I thought that were possible. But I know for a fact he's not coming back. Not ever."

For an instant the marshal's stare narrowed, but he recovered quickly. "I'll give you this. You're awful sure of yourself, son. Cocky is another word that comes to mind. That kind of attitude can come in handy sometimes. This is not one of those times."

"Just trying to establish motive, Marshal."

"You mean mine for wanting Bill Bell dead?"

I held his stare and said nothing.

"Look, if you think I had anything to do with Billy's disappearance—and note I said disappearance, not death—you should speak to my deputy. He's at Rattlesnake Gulch replacing some timbers on the train trestle."

"Is this the deputy who used to be a mall cop?"

"Doesn't mean he can't enforce the law. Pat's okay at what he does. I just have to make sure I don't give him too much responsibility, if you know what I'm saying."

Marshal Buckleberry rose from his chair and walked to the door, signaling our interview was over.

"Marshal, I don't know if this ghost town is going to make it or not, and I don't care. It's obvious you've put a lot of work into it. But one thing's for sure. You have a killer running loose."

Marshal Buckleberry chuckled. "Son, I don't know if your mom and dad and sister are having fun, but I can tell from the way you're going on about this so-called murder, you are. Just remember our agreement. If I get word that our guests are asking about Billy the Kid's disappearance, I'm going to assume it was you that started the rumor, understand?"

"Yes, Marshal."

"Not to mention that if there were a killer running loose like you say, he might want to keep you quiet. Know what I mean?"

I couldn't tell from those sad, hound dog eyes if he was joking or trying to threaten me. I thanked him again for his time and started through the door when he said to me, "You know, son, if you decide to go into law enforcement, count on me as a reference. I'd be happy to vouch for you."

CHAPTER TWELVE
RATTLESNAKE RODEO

I picked up my pony and helmet and trotted up the canyon road in the direction of Rattlesnake Gulch. My pony and I got along fine as long as I let him go at whatever pace suited him. Slow seemed to be his preferred speed.

A mile west of town I turned off the road and made my way up a rutted drive toward a pasture dotted with Black Angus cattle. Salt blocks sat like deformed ice sculptures in open pastureland. Narrow fingers of matted grass showed the way toward a wide watering hole. In a nearby grove the lower branches of some knobby hardwoods had been nibbled clean of leaves. When I reached the railroad tracks, I aimed my trusty steed toward Twilight Tunnel and went clomp-clomping down the middle of the tracks. Maybe a half mile up the tracks I passed the burial mounds. With the morning mist burned off by the heat of the afternoon, the sacred graves looked less imposing. No ethereal spirits beckoning me closer. Maybe the spirits of the Native Americans were taking a siesta. Or were never there in the first place.

My thoughts drifted back to the Bible in my room and the highlighted verses. Were they code? Was someone trying to tip me off as to who the killer was? Or was someone really trying to warn me that ghosts and spirits and demons were real?

I poked my pony into the tunnel and trotted ahead.

About halfway into the tunnel that old saying came to mind: "The light at the end of the tunnel is an oncoming train." I hoped it wasn't, but just to be sure I stopped and listened hard to make sure I didn't hear the Big Sky rumbling toward me. Or racing up from behind. I spurred my pony and he shifted into a full-on trot.

I found the marshal's deputy working on a section of tracks overlooking Rattlesnake Gulch.

Deputy Pat Garrett appeared to be in his early forties and as wide as a linebacker. He stood bent over the rails, wresting a railroad tie from the gravel bed. He'd stripped to the waist, leaving a dark band of sweat around the top of his jeans. Sweat rolled down his sun-browned back, giving his skin the appearance of varnished mahogany. I parked my pony at the bottom of the railroad bed a good ways back from the edge of the gulch. Still, I was close enough to see the muddy river below and take note of the way it had carved away large chunks of earth along the banks. There was enough of a westward tilt to the sun to turn the terra-cotta layers of sand into shades of purple and deep blue.

"Lose your way, cowboy?" Garrett pried off his work gloves and plucked his shirt from a pile of new timbers. With the blue denim sleeve he dried sweat from his wind-chapped cheeks. Scowling, he shouldered into the shirt, snapping the first few buttons.

I expected him to offer his hand but wasn't disappointed when he didn't. Instead, he used it to shade his eyes, giving me a hard look.

"The boy investigating a murder that wasn't."

I said, "Marshal told me I'd find you here."

"Not supposed to be up here except on the train."

"Trying to clear up some confusion about where everyone was yesterday evening."

"He did?" Garrett snapped two more buttons and tucked the hem of his shirt into the waistband of his pants.

"Until just before my family arrived."

"Oh, right. I guess he's talking about when I stopped by his office. We've had some trouble with a bear coming down from the hills and spooking the livestock. I thought the marshal ought to know that I'd checked the perimeter and hadn't seen anything."

"Remember what time you got to his office?"

"Which one? The one on Main Street or that little dumpy trailer he works out of?"

"Whichever one he was working out of just before we arrived."

"That'd be the one on Main Street. Marshal tries to stay

there until around six. That way kids can stop in and get their picture taken in a cell. Makes a good postcard moment. Sometimes he'll run back to the trailer if he needs to do serious work, but that doesn't happen often. About the only crime we have around here is petty theft. Usually turns out someone misplaced their iPod or cell phone."

"Time?" I said again.

He nodded toward a dirt bike resting on its kickstand. "When I'm riding that, it doesn't take long to get around the compound. If I had to guess, I'd say maybe five thirty."

"So the two of you were together until almost six?"

"Sounds about right." I couldn't tell if he was lying to cover for his boss or just giving me the answers I wanted to get me to go away.

He propped the heel of his boot on the pile of timbers and eyed me. "We about done? I need to get back to these ties."

"Almost. How did you hear about the murder?"

"Alleged murder. Marshal said to make sure I didn't call it something it wasn't." Deputy Garrett staked his fists on his hips, arched his back, and stretched. "I think one of the barmaids from the saloon came running over yelling about someone being shot. Stuff like that happens all the time, of course. No big deal. Just part of the drill. But we have to pretend like it matters, so I lit out for the barn."

"You and the marshal?"

"Right. Me and Marshal Buckleberry. I checked the whole first level and didn't see anything. Went into the loft. Nothing. Wandered outside to where you folks were, and the marshal tells me to check again, I guess because you seemed pretty certain there was a body. I hunted all around and found that slug, but that was all."

"The one you pulled from the wall."

"Marshal was upset about that. Said I should've left it for him. But like I said, we don't get too many serious crimes in Deadwood. Certainly nothing like a murder. I just figured someone had been taking target practice up there."

"Who'd want to see Billy dead?"

"Hooo-eee, that's a good one." He massaged the back of his neck with his hand and let his eyes sweep the area around us. "Who'd want Bill dead? Well now, let's see. I guess if I had to say, it'd be…"

But his voice trailed off.

He kept his gaze aimed in my general direction, but his eyes shifted slightly as if he were looking past me. Moving his hand slowly he gripped the shovel handle resting against his hip and lifted it, aiming the blade at my feet. I couldn't figure out what he was doing until I heard the rattler's beaded husk quivering.

I froze. Out of the corner of my eye I saw the snake slither past my foot. Four feet. Maybe longer, though I couldn't be sure because it had begun to coil itself into a knot.

"Don't move, not even an inch. They can sense a change in body temperature. Right now being scared is the absolute wrong reaction."

As if I have another choice.

"You twitch, even a little, and—"

He jabbed the shovel at my legs, striking the dusty ground and flicking his wrist in one swift motion. His thrust of the shovel sent the snake catapulting backwards. It landed with a "whump" and went slithering off under a pile of jumbled timbers.

"Why didn't you kill it?"

"Snakes got a right to live same as us." Garrett put his gloves back on, shouldered the shovel, and trudged up the railbed, stopping next to the tracks. "You were asking about who'd benefit from Bill's death. If I had to guess, I'd say probably that old man at the guardhouse."

"Wyatt Earp? You kidding me? That's guy's a dinosaur."

Garrett scooped a shovel full of gravel from beneath an old timber and tossed it aside. Scoop and toss, scoop and toss, until he'd burrowed a good size trough under the rails. Dropping the shovel, he clamped two gloved hands on the beam and pulled it free.

"Getting old doesn't make a man mellow. Some folks only get meaner. He doesn't have much range as an actor, Earp doesn't. But don't get fooled by that grandfatherly act. Oh he's a charmer, that one is. That's how come the marshal keeps him around. Kids like listening to his stories. He's got all sorts of tales about this place. Some of them are true. But I know for a fact that a few months back Billy caught Earp poking around an abandoned mine. Why, I don't know. Nothing up there except more of these." I followed his gaze and saw another snake slither over rocks and disappear into the brush. "Wouldn't catch me messing around up there in that mine, no sir."

I wasn't sure what he meant. Garrett didn't strike me as the kind of man who scared easily, so I asked him if it was because of the snakes.

He responded with a look of mock surprise. "Rattlers don't

bother me none. Stay out of their way, they'll leave you alone. Fact is, I'm claustrophobic."

He slapped his gloves together, sending a cloud of dust ballooning skyward, and skated down the embankment toward the pile of timber.

"That mine's been off-limits for years," he called out to me. "But that doesn't keep people out. Last summer we caught some kids sneaking up there and having themselves a fine old time. Yes, sir. Cigarette butts, beer cans, liquor bottles. Other things," he said, winking. "Had a young man get bit not more'n twenty feet inside the mine's entrance. Had to medevac him out. Boy nearly lost his leg 'cause of messing around in that shaft."

"So if it's that dangerous, what makes you think Mr. Earp would be up there?"

"Man's a drunk. Claims to have it licked, but a thing like that don't ever stay dead. You can go years without a drink and then one day you take a sip, slip off the wagon, and fall so far and fast they don't find you until the paramedics bring you in with a sheet over your head."

The way he said it made me wonder if Garrett had struggled with drinking himself. Or known someone who had.

"I think that old security guard has been sneaking off when he's supposed to be patrolling the grounds. Him being absent from the guardhouse yesterday when your family arrived wasn't the first time this sort of thing has happened."

The deputy hoisted a new timber on his shoulder and carried it up the hill the way a slugger might carry a bat to home plate.

I asked, "Why haven't you said something?"

"Like I got time to do his job and mine. Marshal fires Earp, that's just more work for me. Here, give me a hand shoving this one in place."

I walked over and knelt beside him, placing my hand on the end of the new lumber. Together we shoved it under the rails.

"No, if you're asking me who has it in for Bill, I'd say start where your vacation began—at the guardhouse. See, what I think happened is that Bill found out about Earp's drinking. Bill's dad was a drunk, and that sort of thing can scare a boy. Maybe Bill confronted Earp. Told him to knock it off or he'd go to the marshal."

"I can't see Mr. Earp killing Billy the Kid over something like that."

"Obviously, you've never been around an out-of-control drunk. They can say and do things a normal person wouldn't dream of doing. Could be Earp took a swing at Billy. Or pulled his gun on Bill. You asked who had a reason to see Bill gone, I'm telling you to talk to Earp. And I bet if you look in that old mine you'll find evidence that old man's been up there taking a drink or two."

"One last thing. That burial mounds place, any truth to the rumor that it's haunted?"

"Boy, you got a wild imagination. No, that's just another of Earp's tall tales. He likes to scare folks that way."

"So all this, the disappearing bank robbers and farmer and that cowboy on the train with his stand-up routine, nothing to it?"

"You know I can't tell you how it's done. But if you're thinking this ghost business is real, you're a worse detective than I am." He wiped his face with a bandana and said to me, "I need to finish this up or else the marshal will think I'm goofing off."

I mounted my pony and turned him toward the tunnel. My list of suspects remained a jumbled lineup of revolving characters. James still looked to be the most likely candidate. He had the most to gain with Billy dead and that gave him motive. Obviously James knew how to handle a pistol. That gave him means. And parking his vehicle in Lazy Jack's put him at the crime scene during the time of the murder.

Garrett had an alibi and no apparent motive, though he had seemed awfully quick to point me in Earp's direction. *Probably bad blood between Garrett and Earp,* I thought. *Or maybe just good detective work by the deputy.*

The elderly security guard seemed like an odd choice for my lead suspect, but Garrett was right about one thing: drinking changes people. Earp's drinking, assuming he was, might be motivation enough. I'd examined cases where people killed for less. And while I hadn't smelled liquor on the guard's breath, that didn't mean he wasn't a closet drinker. I'd learned about that the hard way from my youth baseball coach.

When I had more time and daylight, I'd ride back and check the abandoned mine for signs of Earp's drinking.

I exited the tunnel and found myself thinking of Annie. I didn't want to believe she might be involved in Billy's death, but I couldn't rule her out as a potential suspect either. Her sudden presence at Boot Hill, insistence I not tell the marshal, and reluctance to discuss how she'd received that bruise on her forehead made me wonder if she was hiding something.

Finally, there was Marshal Buckleberry. Money is a powerful motivator, and the marshal had fifty thousand reasons to want Billy dead. I'd watched him nail that bank robber on horseback, and though staged, I had no doubt Buckleberry was a skilled marksman. That left opportunity, and it was clear from Garrett's evasive answers regarding the time he and Buckleberry were together that the deputy was covering for his boss. Probably to keep his job.

One thing was certain. I still had way more questions than answers.

CHAPTER THIRTEEN
GETTING THE LOWDOWN
AT THE HOEDOWN

I returned my pony to its pen and tossed the helmet on the pile. Despite his promise, Marshal Buckleberry had thus far refused to let me inspect the crime scene. Now I'd take a look myself.

I found padlocks on both bay doors. I knew in a few minutes the cook would ring the dinner bell announcing the start of the night's big hoedown at the outdoor pavilion. With luck Annie would be there. I needed to know where she was during the time of the murder. Plus, I sort of missed having her around.

The sky had a coppery pink hue to it. The mountain range cast long shadows across the meadow behind the barn. I knelt beside the padlocked door and inspected the ground. Tire tracks showed where the Charger had pulled away. A second set showed the tread pattern of a large farm tractor. The area around the back of the barn smelled of dusty burlap, diesel fuel, and sawdust. No discernable footprints in the grass or soft dirt leading away. No way in, either.

"Still looking for your ghost?" Wyatt Earp walked around the corner and pointed to tire tracks.

"Where's your horse?" I asked, standing quickly. For a bumbling security guard, he exhibited a stealth-like ability to sneak up on people. "Marge, is it?"

"Good memory. Put her away for the night. Any luck finding your missing body?"

I wondered if he was fishing. His question seemed innocent enough, but after Deputy Garrett's comments, I now had a new appreciation for the cunning of the elderly security guard.

I brushed dirt from my knees. "You named her after your wife. That's why I was able to remember. And no, I haven't found Billy the Kid's body. But I will."

"That's good. For you, I mean, not Bill. Or the people of Deadwood. If it turns out you do uncover a murder, the press will be all over this place, asking questions, digging into people's pasts. Could uncover some skeletons. Some folks wouldn't like that."

I was tempted to tell him I'd heard about his drinking but instead I said, "You have a key to Marshal Buckleberry's office? Not the one on Main Street, but the trailer?"

"Maybe. Why?"

"The marshal said I could borrow his computer to access

the Internet. I would ask him myself but he seems to be dodging me."

"I don't know. The marshal is kind of funny about his deputies being in his office when he's not around. You may think he's just a two-bit actor playing the part of an Old West peace officer, but he's actually a pretty good lawman."

"Won't take but a few minutes. You can stand over my shoulder and watch."

"Guess it'd be okay if it helps you solve your case. Young buck like you we need to keep occupied. Otherwise you might get into some real trouble."

"Don't really see how a computer is going to help you solve a crime," Earp said, looking over my shoulder. "But then, I never have understood them contraptions anyway. I took a course at a community college a few years back. Mostly it was senior citizens like myself trying to learn how to check email. Didn't help me much. Kept forgetting my password. I still like talking on the phone. And not one of them cell phones that you can't hear on, neither, but a real, honest-to-goodness landline with a speaker and receiver.

The computer monitor flashed and began scrolling data.

Earp asked, "What's next?"

"We wait for the program to crunch the information I entered. When it's done it'll spit out a list of the most likely suspects."

"Crunch what?"

"The program will evaluate the names, motives, and means I entered and sort it all into a report that'll make sense. It's all done with a mathematical formula. I could try to explain it, but if you didn't understand how computers and email work, I doubt this would be any easier."

"Do you need to be here in the office for it to work?"

I explained how the software application resided on a server in a bunker farm outside McLean, Virginia. That produced a big chuckle.

"Hold on, now. You telling me there's a whole farm with nothing but computers in the field?"

"That's just what it's called, a bunker farm. It's a large industrial building without windows. Nothing inside but computer servers and wires and routers, switches and hubs."

Earp stared blankly at me. "So basically them computers do the investigating for you."

The screen refreshed and displayed another login form. I entered a new ID and password and hit enter.

"They don't investigate anything," I replied. "All they do is run the program that analyzes the data. It's still up to me to review the final report and determine the most likely suspect."

"I still don't see how computers on a farm can know anything 'bout what's going on in Deadwood Canyon."

I tried a new approach. "You remember the old TV show Columbo?"

"Sure do. With him it was always, 'Just one more thing.' Sort of like you."

"Okay, well, a bunch of us in our online detective group took all those episodes plus hundreds of other cop and detective shows and cataloged every murder. Then we took the crime, suspects, motives, and facts of the case and entered that information into a database. Turns out a lot of crime shows use real police cases. By using the shows, we can overlay a real case, like this one, and come up with a pretty good summary of who the real killer is."

"Who is 'we'?"

"Members of Cybersleuths. It's a closed membership of amateur detectives who look at real unsolved murders and *help* law enforcement agencies solve crimes. Of course, not everyone appreciates our efforts."

"You mean like you butting in where you're not wanted."

"Exactly."

"And all you have to do is look at a piece of paper and announce the killer."

"It's not quiet that easy. But it's not as hard as you might think. For example, did you know there are over seven television episodes almost identical to this one? Murders where theatrics and fake killings lead to a real murder?"

"Don't say."

"That's why I've been interviewing anyone who might have had access to the barn yesterday afternoon. Without a body I can't get an autopsy report and without that, I don't know the time of death. But it'll work out. In the meantime, I'll let the other members of our group review the evidence while I'm digging around here."

From outside, a dinner bell clanged. Earp lifted the window shade and looked out. "You said this program on that funny computer farm runs all by itself? Don't need you standing around watching it, is that right?"

I nodded.

"Then I say we go grab dinner before the marshal comes back and catches us."

I typed a short message to our system administrator telling him I'd log back on later, then killed the browser window, erased my browsing history, and put the marshal's computer back into sleep mode. Earp made sure the door was locked and led me down the steps toward the covered walkway.

"Mind if I ask you something?" I said in a casual way. "Last night in my room I found a Bible. Several verses had been underlined or highlighted. All of them dealt with ghosts or made references to dead people coming back from the grave. At first I thought the killer … or someone else wanted me to find those verses. Like maybe they were clues. But then I wondered if maybe it was just me reading too much into things. Could be whoever stayed in my room before me highlighted those passages because they found them interesting."

"What are you trying to ask, son?"

"I know you mentioned this morning how some people think the Native American burial ground is haunted. But you never said yourself if you believe in that sort of thing. You've worked in this ghost town a long time. What's your take on spirits returning from the dead?"

He removed his hat and rubbed his hand through his thick white hair. We'd stopped next to a streetlight casting a halo of light onto Main Street. Kerosene lamps flickered in shop windows. On the second story balcony of the hotel, guests leaned against the railing, enjoying the coolness of dusk. Horses tied to hitching posts and the banging of the piano in the saloon made the scene feel … well, special. Like I'd stepped back in time.

I fell in step with Earp and we headed out of town, walking toward the corral and stables.

"Got a friend of mine who lives in Roswell, New Mexico," said Mr. Earp. "Swears a little green man from outer space served him a plate of fried eggs at Kenny's Diner. 'Course he's also the same buddy who believes Elvis is living in the catacombs of Disney World. Says he's got pictures of The King peeking up from a manhole. He also claims all this global warming business is a government conspiracy to get us to stop using automobiles and go back to riding horses. Says there's a whole secret program set up to keep the herds hidden until Congress bans cars. He's a lot like you. Spends way too much time on that Internet thing."

"My sister is sure she's seen a ghost. She says when we die that's it. No heaven or hell. We only end up wandering the earth looking for our bodies."

"Sounds like a pretty bleak outlook on the future if you ask me."

"My point exactly. If you can conjure up enough faith to believe in ghosts, why is it so hard to believe there's something else after we die?"

Earp grew quiet. I could tell he was thinking, so I kept quiet, waiting while we strolled past the last of the buildings toward the little white church at the end of town.

At last Earp said, "For a long time I never gave this life after death business much thought. Just went about my business thinking this was all there was. Then Marge got sick and I fell into a place where ... well, let's just say I needed something more than my own smarts to get me through. Talked to a lot of folks. Some of them with lots of letters after their names. They tried to convince me that whatever I believed was fine so long as it made me feel better. That sort of talk sounded like a bunch of hogwash. I did a little digging and reading on my own and settled on the thing that made the most sense to me. I may not be college educated, but I know you can't just head off down a road and expect it to take you someplace it ain't going."

We'd reached the little chapel. Earp stopped and rested his boot on the front steps, his eyes gazing upwards at the stars winking on and off and the steeple slanted against the night sky.

"Some folks say we're cursed. Made a wrong turn long time ago and we're still paying for our mistake. Maybe we are. But if we are cursed, I hope we get a second or third chance. God knows I could use 'em."

"So ... ghosts. Real or not?"

"I wish I could tell you for certain, but I plain don't know. Every man's got to find truth on his own. That's what my Marge used to tell me."

Behind the church, torch lights glowed brightly. Bales of hay framed the entrance to the path leading down to the pavilion. Guests mingled, waiting to board the wagon that would take them to the bonfire built near the small pond. Somewhere beyond the flickering torch lights a country band played square dance music.

Earp peeled off as if he were going back to town, then paused and said to me, "The other day you asked me why I wasn't at the guardhouse when you arrived. I told you I had to reset the security. I did, but that wasn't the only reason. I plum forgot to mention that I stopped by the marshal's office on my way back. He radioed and said he needed help moving a filing cabinet. He showed up about fifteen minutes after I did. Said he'd got tied up taking care of some things. We wrestled that cabinet over to behind his desk, just where he wanted it."

"You're talking about his office on Main Street, right?"

Earp shook his head. "Trailer office. Back where we were. That's why he wanted it moved. Every time he opened the bottom drawer it raked over the power strip. Kept accidentally cutting off his computer."

My mind raced as I tried to make sense of what Earp had just said. The marshal claimed he and Deputy Garrett were together just before Billy the Kid was shot. And Pat Garrett had confirmed that the two of them were in the office on Main Street when my family arrived. But I also recalled how Garrett had acted confused when I'd first mentioned Buckleberry's alibi. I wondered if the deputy was so desperate to keep his job that he'd be willing to lie for the marshal.

Pointing through the trees toward the train depot, Earp said, "All this talking about dying and Marge has left me feeling a little sorry for myself. Think I'll do a little walking by myself, if that's okay."

I said it was and strolled down the path toward the pavilion. Outdoor lights shaped to look like lanterns hung from dusty rafter beams. Checkered tablecloths covered picnic tables. A fiddle player stood on a small stage at one end of the open-sided building. Pulling his bow across the strings, he nodded to a banjo player and the picking and plucking commenced.

I snagged a cup of punch and spied Annie standing in the shadows just beyond the spray of lantern lights. She wore a knee-length denim skirt, white blouse, and calf-high cowgirl boots. Jesse James leaned close to her, his cowboy boots moving to the music. I got the impression he was trying to get her to dance with him.

She slowly shook her head and turned as if to walk away. When she did, James grabbed her roughly by the elbow and spun her around. When he saw me marching toward them, he released Annie and hurried off toward the stand of trees.

"What was that all about?" I asked.

Annie, ignoring the question, said, "Is that drink for me?" She drained the cup and nodded toward my parents seated at a long picnic table near the hay bales. "Mind if I eat with you and your family? Great," she exclaimed, hurrying toward our table.

"Sure," I replied. "But I should warn you. We're not your typical dysfunctional family. We're worse."

"At least you have a family. Come on. Let's get in line before all the barbeque is gone."

I grabbed a plastic plate and silverware and said in a low voice, "My parents argue. A lot."

"I wish I had parents who argued," Annie shot back.

"Speaking of arguing," I said. "What were you and James talking about?"

"Nothing."

"You sure? Looked pretty heated to me."

"He's just that way. Really, it was nothing."

"Is he the one we saw last night on Boot Hill? Is that what you two were arguing about?"

"Don't you ever talk about anything else?"

"Cars. I like talking about them, sometimes." I skipped the salad bar and green beans and went for a double helping of chipped beef. "You need to be careful," I told her. "James is a lot more dangerous than you think."

"And *you* need to be careful about assuming things about people without proof."

"Come on, Annie. Tell me who you saw in the graveyard last night."

She dropped a roll on her plate. "I … can't."

"Can't or won't?"

"Forget I said anything about it, please. Otherwise—"

"What? Did he threaten to hit you again?"

"Jess? No! You seriously need to get your facts straight before you end up looking even more foolish than you already do."

"What's that supposed to mean?"

"Nothing. Let's just drop it."

"Don't forget, Annie. You saw the body too!"

"No, all I saw was some man burying something. I thought I might know who it was. I was mistaken."

I felt my cheeks grow warm. "You're lying."

"I am not! I honestly don't know. I thought I did but I don't."

"Fine. At least tell me who you *think* you saw last night in the graveyard. Was it James? Your uncle? Wyatt Earp?"

She whirled, glaring at me. "You know what your problem

is, Nick Caden? You've let this detective stuff go to your head. You've become convinced there really *was* a murder."

"What happened to you at the corral this morning, Annie?"

"Nothing happened. I mean, nothing except I fell off my horse, which, by the way, wasn't the first time. You know the reason I was there last night? In the graveyard? I thought it would be fun to tag along. This place is, like, so boring. I mean, your family and the other guests might think it's cool, but day after day of the same stunts and skits and it's like, gag me with a spoon. Anyway, I thought with you ... well, it's not important."

"Come on. Tell me."

"Jess was right about you. You *are* weird. And a little obsessive-compulsive."

"Oh, so now you're taking his side?"

She pushed her tray down the line and placed a cup of tea next to her plate. "I'm not taking anybody's side. But since you're probably going to keep badgering me until I tell you— the thing we were arguing about was you."

"Me?"

"Jess thinks you're weird. I was trying to stand up for you. But I swear, it's getting harder and harder. Do you know what Uncle Walt told me today? He said you accused him of murder. The town marshal! How crazy is that? Is there anyone you don't suspect?"

She pivoted and headed toward the staff table.

I said, "I thought you were sitting with me and my family."

"Changed my mind."

"Oh great. Leave. Go on! That's what you're good at. Starting stuff and not finishing."

She marched back, slammed her tray down, and barked, "You want to know why Jess dragged me over there? What we were *really* talking about? He had something he wanted to tell me. Something important. Said it might help with your stupid investigation. When I got all excited and asked him what it was, he started laughing at me. Told me he was only trying to find out how much of your stupid murder mystery theory I actually believed."

"So he didn't really have anything to add to the case?"

"Oh for crying out loud. Don't you get it? There is no case! No murder!"

Others turned and stared, causing her to blush.

"Oh there's a case, all right," I said in a low voice. "And if you want, after dinner I'll let you in on who I think the killer is."

"How could you possibly know that? Jess told me himself that Bill is in L.A. My uncle told me the same thing."

"Meet me outside your uncle's office after dinner, and I'll show you how I know."

CHAPTER FOURTEEN
BOOT UP AND BOOTED OUT

"**M**y uncle would kill me if he knew I was letting you into his office."

"Don't use that word," I replied, taking a moment to warm my hands. "He's on my suspect list."

"I'm not surprised."

We stood outside the marshal's office, shivering in the cool night air. I couldn't believe how quickly the temperature dropped, but Annie explained that part of it was the high elevation. We huddled on the stoop while Annie worked her key into the lock, jiggling it until the knob turned.

"Am I?" she said, pushing the door open. "On your list of suspects?"

"Of course. Now please hurry before someone sees us. Or I freeze."

I followed her inside, and she switched on the desk lamp. "He keeps his user password…"

"On a sticky note, I know," I said as I stepped around her. I pulled out the keyboard drawer and hit the enter key, bringing the computer out of sleep mode. Dropping into Buckleberry's chair, I began to type while Annie leaned over my shoulder.

"Wow, you're fast."

"I've done this so often it's become habit," I said, waiting for the page to load. "But I have to be careful because if I key in the wrong ID and password more than twice, the program will blacklist my IP address and lock me out of the system."

The screen changed. A long stream of text populated the center column.

"I don't understand; none of those words make any sense."

"What you're seeing is a statistical analysis showing the highest probability of who might have killed Billy the Kid."

"I'm seeing what?"

"The list of likely suspects."

"Oh." She leaned closer to the screen. "So I *am* on the list."

"Yes, but not too high. See?" I said, pointing to her name.

"But why am I listed at all?"

"You work here. You carry a gun. I haven't asked if you have an alibi for yesterday afternoon and don't know if you have motive. That might change your ranking."

"Lucky me."

"You're rated low because you're female and young."

"And that helps me why?"

"Because Billy was killed in a violent act. Males are more likely to use brute force. Statistics show males are more likely to shoot, strangle, stab, or bludgeon their victims. Females, on the other hand, are more inclined to use poison to kill their victims. It's also true that males are significantly more likely to kill strangers than are females, and that females kill family members more often than males."

"So if you're a married guy and you make your wife mad, watch what you eat."

"Exactly."

"Wow. You really do know a lot about this. So your list, it's ranked in order?" I nodded. "And you have Jess at the top?"

"Not me. The program. Based on comparable crimes where suspects of a similar nature had means, motive, and opportunity, your buddy Jesse James would be considered the primary person of interest. Due to the nature of this particular murder, the program is weighted in favor of motivation."

"What do you mean 'nature of this murder'? How would Bill's death be different from any other crime?"

"It probably wasn't a crime of passion. Evidence points to a calculated and planned assassination."

"Because…?"

"Of the single gunshot wound to the chest, the lack of evidence at the crime scene, and the fact that nothing was taken from the victim that we know of. A crime of passion would have been messier. Blood splatters, footprints, clothes fibers. You see something like what happened to Billy the Kid and it suggests the murderer killed for money, power, or revenge, not passion. More than likely the killer took his time sanitizing the crime scene. Not that I've had a chance to see for myself. Your uncle hasn't let me."

"But it could possibly change your assumptions of the case if you were able to examine the *supposed* crime scene, right?"

"Wouldn't hurt, but it's not necessary. Remember, I'm not trying to solve the case based on the actual evidence. What I mean is, I'm not building a case for the prosecution. What I'm doing is pulling together the list of suspects and letting the program determine who the killer is. That information, plus the fact that most of the time the program is correct, saves the real detectives and the prosecuting attorney a lot of time."

"But what if your program is wrong and they arrest the wrong person?"

"The Cyberslueth program has a fail-safe feature built in that runs a scan against wrongful convictions. Once the authorities have the suspect in custody and all the evidence has been gathered, we run the scan. Most wrongful convictions come from over-aggressive detectives and prosecuting attorneys anxious to get a win. If those working within the system would take their time, analyze the data, and rely less on eyewitness testimony, fewer innocent men and women would go to prison. Not to mention there would be fewer criminals roaming the streets. Like here."

Annie stared at the monitor. "You weren't kidding. You really *do* have Uncle Walt on that list."

"After James, yes. But you can see his rating isn't anywhere near that of your friend Jess. There's only a 42 percent likelihood the marshal is the killer."

"Looks like you have every staff member in town listed."

"All that I could identify. Can you do me a favor and make sure that printer is powered on?" I nodded toward the metal stand behind the desk. A hulking, ancient dot-matrix printer crouched on a wobbly metal table. "I'd like to study this back in my room tonight."

"Wyatt Earp has a drinking problem? How would *you* know?"

"I put in what I learn and what people tell me. Doesn't make it true."

She pressed a button and the printer began to hum.

"So what's next? Are you going to tell Uncle Walt to arrest Jess?"

"Not until we recover the body. Once we get the ballistic report on the slug found in the barn ..." I hesitated, wondering if I should mention the other slug I'd found in my pocket, but I decided against it.

"You were saying?"

"Right, after the ballistic report, I'll need to find the murder weapon. From there we call in the coroner to perform an autopsy on the body. That'll tell us everything we need to know about how Billy was killed. Hopefully, then the authorities will take it and follow up from there."

Due to the whirring of the printer and my own excited yapping, I'd failed to hear the trailer door open. I'd been so eager to impress Annie with my knowledge that I didn't even notice the marshal standing in the doorway until I felt the rush of cool air enter the room.

"Er—Marshal?"

Buckleberry stared stone-faced at Annie. "Him, I'm not surprised. But you? Sneaking into my office? Get out. Both of you."

"In a minute," I mumbled. "Need to get—"

"OUT!" roared the marshal. "I never expected this, young lady. What would your mother think if she found out her daughter was caught breaking and entering."

"Technically, I didn't break anything," Annie answered. "I just—"

"Do you think because you're family you can have the run of the place?"

The marshal held out his hand. Annie pulled the office key from her skirt pocket and sheepishly walked past the marshal.

I used the momentary distraction to kill the browser window and my session on our server. With a click of the mouse I deleted my browsing history.

"We're not finished talking about this, Annie."

She gave me a quick, guilty look, then pulled the door shut behind her.

"And you," Buckleberry said to me. "I thought I made it clear you were only to use my computer when I was with you." The marshal's eyes narrowed into slits no wider than a snake's. Anything I said would only prolong the sermon, so I remained silent and tried to look penitent. *Penitent: that was one of the words on my AP English exam. Means "sorry, remorseful, or contrite."* I was none of those, but needed this to blow over so I could get back to my room and study the report.

"Be thankful I'm not going to file charges. I should. This is serious, you being in here like this."

"Yes, sir."

I wanted to tell him that I would have been glad to wait to use his computer, but he had been so busy calling instructions to square dancers that I didn't want to bother him. Problem was, I hadn't wanted him watching over my shoulder while I reviewed the results.

"Sorry, Marshal. Wasn't sure you'd ever get around to letting me use the computer. You said I could visit the crime scene, but that hasn't happened yet either."

"Been busy trying to do my job. But it's getting harder with you fouling things up. Like this." He held up a computer cable as though unsure where it went.

"Sorry. I guess I accidently bumped it loose." I took the USB cable from him and plugged it into the front of the computer.

"But don't forget, Marshal. You asked me to investigate a murder and that's what I'm doing. Maybe you thought you were humoring me. Or maybe you were trying to keep Mom and Dad off your back. But the more I learn, the easier it is for me to believe that any one of you could have killed Billy."

"Fine. I have no problem with you having hunches and following leads. That's all well and good. But don't you ever let me catch you in my office again without my permission, do you understand?"

"Yes, sir."

"Now get out." He snatched the report from the printer and handed it to me. "And take this with you."

CHAPTER FIFTEEN
GLORY HOLE

The alarm on my cell went off at five in the morning. I dressed quickly and hurried to the corral where I found a middle-aged ranch hand with lizard-brown skin climbing from the cab of a pickup. I intercepted him on his way to the stables, and when we reached the stalls, I pointed to my pony.

"No, señor," he said apologetically.

I placed my hands together as though praying and said with a huge smile on my face, "Pony, please?"

He exhaled loudly, making it sound like he was doing me a huge favor. Strapping a saddle onto my pony, he handed me a helmet. I declined, hopped on, and off I rode at a fast walk. I followed the same route as before, making my way toward

Rattlesnake Gulch and the burial grounds. I had sat up past midnight reviewing the summary of the case, and I now knew with certainty who killed Billy the Kid. One new wrinkle bothered me, though, and that was Annie's behavior at the dance last night.

There had been tension between her and James, but not the sort I expected between a brawler and his victim. More like a high school couple having a tiff. But if James didn't hit Annie, who did? And if James *was* the man who'd attacked us in the graveyard, then why hadn't she shown more fear? Did I have the wrong suspect at the top of my list? Or were the two of them in it together?

I reached the train tracks and crossed over, guiding my pony through the thicket and toward the burial mounds. A smudge of mist clung to the ground. As before, the fog hovered primarily over the burial site. And, as before, vapors wafted into the air. A chill crept its way down my back. Earp's words came back to me: *Wish I could tell you for sure there wasn't any such thing as ghosts.*

A short way past the mounds, I crossed over a ridge and followed a trail down to the Hole in the Wall Junction and the abandoned mine. I knew I'd found the path because the sign read:

TRIAL LEADING TO THE ABANDONED MIND.

Apparently this *trail* was a *trial* for the *mind* of the person responsible for making *mine* signs.

The trail circled around the back of the water tower and up a steep ridge, dumping me onto a wide, level area littered with rusty tools. A weathered gray shack tilted severely to one side not more than fifty feet from a man-sized mouse hole cut into the mountain. Large boulders from a fresh rockslide covered one half of the entrance. On a discarded pile of lumber someone had tossed a wooden sign spray-painted with the word "CLOSD."

I scanned the rocky crags of the mesa towering above me. The first rays of dawn brushed the tips of the mountains, turning them purple. *Majestic, just like the song says.* Circling overhead, a hawk searched the valley floor for jackrabbits and prairie dogs and slow-footed mice. I crept closer to the entrance, hesitating. I had no intention of going too far into the mine—only enough to see for myself if Pat Garrett's claim was true. *Find evidence that Mr. Earp's been drinking on the job and I've got motive. Not much of one, but motive nonetheless.*

I pulled my Streamlight Stinger flashlight from my jacket pocket and, taking a deep breath, crawled over the debris of dirt and rocks.

The air inside felt noticeably cooler and carried the musty odor of dampness. I followed the shaft back a good twenty feet before coming to a larger cavern. Aiming my Streamlight, I swept the beam across the chamber floor, up the walls, and overhead. Stalactites covered the ceiling, their pointed fangs aimed downward as if the cave were the mouth of a large beast preparing to snap shut. Bits of broken glass, snack food wrappers, and crumpled beer cans lay scattered about. At the far reach of the Streamlight's beam, a pair of narrow-gauge metal rails curved away into darkness. Next to the track, a wooden pushcart lay tipped on its side. Based on the tracks and size of the chamber, the area had probably served as the main staging area for miners.

I paused, listening for the heavy breathing of a furry beast or the husky rattle of a snake. Mr. Earp had warned of a brown bear prowling the area; Deputy Garrett of snakes. I had no desire to encounter either. Certainly not in here.

My eyes adjusted to the muted light seeping into the shaft. Damp walls displayed a mosaic pattern of sand and clay and salt sediment sandwiched between the wider areas of limestone. Perfect for "glory holes"—those large pockets pressed into the strata where veins of gold deposits lay waiting.

The hole on the far wall looked to be about eighteen inches high. I stepped closer and aimed my light inside. Someone had used the cavity to deposit trash. Fast food bags, amber beer bottles, and empty cigarette packs. *Something else in there, too. Something shiny and long.* I reached in, brushing aside the bottles and fingered the cold, hard barrel of a ...

"What are *you* doing here?"

I spun, my skin warming as adrenaline surged. Annie stood behind me, her figure silhouetted against the dull light of dawn spilling into the mine.

"I could ask you the same thing."

"We need to get out of here," she urged. "This mine isn't safe. Didn't you see the sign?"

"Speaking of that, who *is* in charge of signage?" I asked, smirking.

"You're looking at her. Why? Is something wrong?"

"I should've guessed."

"What's that supposed to mean?"

"Just that you need to get a dictionary."

"And you need to get out before ..."

We both pivoted at once, gawking at the entrance.

"Yeah, I heard it too," I said, moving closer to her.

Someone or *something* was prowling around. I saw its shape dart past, heard the clatter of rocks rolling away. Annie snuggled up close. I clicked off my Streamlight and together we stood in darkness, waiting.

"Bear?" she asked, her voice shaky.

"Maybe."

Abandoned mine; bear den. Death trap.

Whatever it was pawed about, crunching loose rocks. We backed toward the overturned pushcart and stood in the shadows. I wasn't sure how we would outrun a bear—if it *was* a bear.

"You didn't answer me," Annie said, her voice barely audible. "What are you doing in here?"

"Checking a lead. You?"

"Had a hunch."

A lumbering shape moved back across the opening. *Definitely big enough to be a bear.*

"Yeah, right," I countered. "You're afraid of what I'll find, aren't you?"

"Oh, please. You're the one who should be worried."

But before I could ask her why, the grunting and shuffling grew into a rumble. Together we watched as the entrance collapsed, turning off the day.

"Nick?"

I chanced it and flicked on the light. I found the entrance filled in with rocks and dirt. A fine mist of dust rolled toward us.

Annie's hand found mine and squeezed.

I said, "Don't suppose there's another way out?"

I felt her shudder and knew there wasn't.

We stood in silence for several seconds before I said as calmly as I could, "Don't panic. We'll find a way out. This can't be the only way into this mine."

"Panic? Who's panicking? You see me panicking? Do I *look* like I'm panicking? I'm not panicking."

"This isn't as bad as it looks."

"Sure looks bad. In fact, bad never looked so good. Bad would be an improvement. You know what this is? This is cataclysmic."

"I think you meant catastrophic."

"I *know* what word I meant even if I can't spell it. Cataclysmic means devastating, disastrous, and dreadful, and that's what this is, only much worse!" Her voice had crept up to a shriek. I could sense a quickening of her breathing and knew she was losing it.

I took a deep breath, coughed out some dust, and decided to change tactics. "Who's trying to kill us, Annie?"

"Boy, you find conspiracies everywhere, don't you? Who's trying to kill us? That's funny. You. That's who's trying to kill us. You're the real villain, sneaking up here where you're not supposed to be."

"Hang on a second," I shot back. "What just happened wasn't an accident. Somebody wanted to trap us in here."

"Give me a break. I warned you the mine was unsafe. There's a sign that even says so. That's why I came here. To tell you to leave."

"That thing we saw out there prowling around the entrance, it wasn't a bear."

"How do *you* know?"

"I don't *know*. But a bear, at least a brown one, has a strong odor, almost like a skunk. I didn't smell anything like that."

"Maybe you don't smell as well as you think."

"You saying I stink?"

"You know what I mean."

I sniffed. The dust-filled air delivered a whiff of Annie's scented shampoo, which actually smelled pretty nice. I was afraid at any moment she'd start thinking about how we were going to get out and *if* we would get out, so in an attempt to keep her from wigging out, I said, "Apple blossom, right?"

"Huh?"

"Your shampoo."

"So you can tell what type of shampoo I use, big deal."

"Just saying, it smells nice is all."

"Think we should start screaming? I'll start."

"Wait! First tell me who sent you up here?"

"Nobody. I decided to come on my own."

"Okay, if not *sent*, then who *suggested* you follow me up here?"

"I don't get you. Why can't I just be concerned about you? How come you're always questioning my motives?"

"I dunno. It's just what I do. Who told you I'd be here?"

"No one. Nobody told me you'd be here."

"You sure?"

She sighed impatiently. "Fine. It was Jess, okay? He said there was something in here I needed to see. Something I would find interesting. Satisfied?"

"*He* knows you're here?"

"Doubt it. But that's what the two of us were discussing last night just before you arrived at the pavilion. He was telling me about something in the mine I needed to see. Then we got off on you and this dumb murder case and … well, you walked up before I could find out what he wanted me to find up here."

"Well for once both of you might be telling the truth."

"Might?"

"Here, look at this."

I led her across the room toward the glory hole and aimed the Streamlight so she could see inside.

"An empty whisky bottle in a paper sack?" she said, frowning. "I think Jess was talking about something else."

"Not the bottle," I replied matter-of-factly. "Behind it. The shiny thing. Careful, though. There might be a …"

The black snake slithered out from the bag and dropped onto the ground. It couldn't have been more than a foot long, but it might as well have been a python given Annie's reaction. She was clear on the other side of the cave before I could turn around to tell her it was nonvenomous.

"Don't you want to see the thing I was pointing at?" I said, grinning. "I bet this is what James wanted you to find."

"No!"

"Oh come on. There can't be two snakes in there."

"You look."

"But I already know what it is."

"Why? Did you put it there?"

"Me? No. But I have a pretty good idea who did."

I reached in and pulled the gun out.

The Schofield felt heavy in my hand. Elaborate scrollwork

covered the nickel-plated barrel, cylinder, and trigger guard, giving the piece a plastic, toy-like appearance. But there was nothing childish about the weapon. Using the bandana I'd tucked in my back pocket, I gloved the weapon and held it in my right hand. With a flick of my wrist, I swung the frame down, exposing the cylinder.

One empty chamber. I sniffed and detected the faint odor of gunpowder. I knew from the book I'd purchased at the general store that the eight-inch barrel, like the one on this gun, dampened the muzzle kick and improved accuracy. This model had a tiny notch in front of the trigger, a missing screw on the butt plate, and the initials W.E. etched into the underside of the barrel near the trigger guard. Ballistics would be able to tell me if the gun had been fired recently, but the missing bullet already suggested it had.

If the slug found in the barn matched the markings on the barrel, then the gun I held was probably the one that killed Billy the Kid.

"Now why would your friend Jess send you up here to find this?" I asked for Annie's benefit.

"Maybe to prove he didn't kill anyone."

I told Annie about my conversation with Earp and how James had asked to borrow his revolver. How James claimed he couldn't find a gun at Lazy Jack's.

"So now do you believe he's innocent?" she demanded. "That Jess couldn't have had anything to do with whatever it is you think he did?"

"Oh, it's possible Jesse James is telling the truth—that Earp fed me that line because he'd already killed Billy the Kid and dropped the gun off in here. Mr. Earp was away from his guardhouse around the time of the murder, so it's possible. By the way, did you know Earp has a drinking problem?"

"Had. *Had* a problem. My uncle said he kicked it years ago."

"The addiction must've kicked back. This empty whisky bottle. James hinting there was something in here for you to find. Wyatt Earp's gun. Doesn't look good for the old man."

"I'll tell you what doesn't look good," Annie declared. "US DYING IN HERE!"

"Don't worry. I'm sure my parents are looking for us. Probably on their way up here right now," I said hopefully. "I'm betting the guy who loaned me the pony has already shown them which way I rode off. We'll be found."

"Yes, but when?"

I didn't want to tell her my real fear, which was that we'd suffocate first. "Soon enough," I answered casually. "In the meantime, let's see if we can find an air vent. All mines have 'em."

"Lead the way. The further we get away from that snake the better."

CHAPTER SIXTEEN
BODILY HARM

I marked our place of departure by scratching an X on the wall. If my parents or the marshal came looking for us, I wanted them to know we were alive. I took Annie's hand and aimed my light down the narrow passageway. For a moment I pictured the two of us lying dead on the floor, our fingers raw from trying to claw our way out. My anger grew as I thought of someone, Jesse James probably, smugly waiting outside the cave entrance for us to cry out. I made up my mind I wouldn't give him that satisfaction. The clues to Billy the Kid's death lay with the revolver tucked into the waistband of my pants. Now all I had to do was get out alive and deliver the evidence to Marshal Buckleberry.

The rusty rails curved around and down the tunnel. We proceeded cautiously, with Annie never falling more than a half step behind me. I'd only gone a few feet when I etched another X on the wall. A few feet further, another. Three dots make a line, and I didn't want there to be any question as to the direction we'd gone. Plus, the marks would make it easy to find our way back.

The Streamlight's beam illuminated an intersection of tunnels. One curving to our right, the other blocked by rubble. Clasping Annie's hand tighter, we jogged toward the junction, stopped, and listened. Far off I thought I heard the call of a hawk.

"This way," I whispered, and pulled her deeper into the mine.

With the cart rails behind us, I knew we'd taken a side shaft, one not normally used by the miners. My hope was that the tunnel had the air vent we needed. My hopes faded when we rounded a corner and came to a dead end. Nothing but stone walls beside and ahead of us.

"Now what?" Annie asked in a quivering voice.

I clicked off the flashlight and stared at the darkness, listening. *Maybe we missed the vent*, I thought, looking over my shoulder. The density of blackness became more than Annie could stand, and I heard her beginning to sob softly. Releasing her hand, I moved my arm around her waist and pulled her close.

Then I saw it. The faintest sliver of silver shimmering about a foot above eye level. My fingers felt the cold stone wall and worked their way up. I turned the Streamlight back on.

"Hold this," I told Annie, passing her the flashlight. "I'll hoist you up and you aim that light into the gap."

I bent down and she stepped into my cupped hands as though slipping her boot into the stirrups of her saddle. I lifted her up and said, "Well?"

"Sorry, Nick. But I don't see anything."

"How far back does it go?"

"I don't know. And I don't want to stick my hand in there to find out. But it looks like only a few feet like that other shelf we saw where you found the gun."

I set her down, took the light from her, and we returned to the main tunnel.

"We'll never get out of here, will we?" she said.

"Sure we we will," I replied, trying to sound hopeful. "Let's keep going this way. We're bound to find the end soon."

And we did. About fifty steps ahead, the rails stopped in a chamber littered with crumpled beer cans, broken bottles, and an assortment of abandoned mining tools.

"What is that?" Annie asked, pointing to chalky splotches on the floor.

I directed the Streamlight at the milky smears, then gradually moved the beam up the wall toward the ceiling. Annie shrieked. I might have too if I hadn't been tipped off by the dusty covering of feces on the floor.

Bats, hundreds of them, hanging like darts, their pointed ears erect, began emitting squeaky bat noises in response to Annie's screams.

I clamped my hand over her mouth. "Please," I whispered to her. "Don't get them excited." I kept the light aimed at the ceiling but watched Annie's eyes. "We good? Can I remove my hand?"

She nodded.

I let go.

"I told you, never do that again," she hissed.

"And you need to stop freaking out. They're just b—"

"Bats that can give us rabies."

"Actually, bats are more like birds," I replied. "They feed off pollen. The idea that bats prey on humans is an urban myth. The vampire bats of South America are the only bats that drink blood, and even then they prefer livestock, not people."

"And this is supposed to comfort me how?"

"Means we're near an opening someplace."

"Unless their 'out' is the main entrance." She jerked her head toward another rail cart. This one sat on the rails beside the wall. "What does a bat eat when it's trapped, anyway?"

"Not sure."

"Then I think we've reached the end of the line and should head back."

"Not yet we haven't."

I wanded the light to my left and pointed to the wooden ladder protruding from the floor. Annie followed me over and together we peered into the hole. Below us, maybe ten feet down, was a second level. The flooring looked to be covered in dirt, which I took to be a good sign.

I pulled Annie away from the hole and positioned her in the center of the room directly beneath the bats. I handed her the flashlight and said, "Stand here and keep shining this light."

"Why? What are you going to do?"

"I need to know how far back we are from the main entrance."

Before she could argue, I jogged away, retracing our steps. The Streamlight's beam reached farther than I'd expected. I was almost back to the main entrance before I had to slow to keep from stumbling over the rough floor. Finally I reached the glory hole and bent forward, panting. With hands resting on my knees I calculated the distance. *Forty-six seconds. Plenty of time to race back if someone calls to us.* I took one final check of the entrance and returned to Annie.

We descended the ladder and landed in another, smaller chamber. Support beams bracketed an opening that was maybe chest high on me.

"How long do we keep exploring before we head back?" she asked nervously, eyeing the tapered shaft.

"Back?"

"Once the batteries die, that's it. I don't want to try walking back in the dark. Especially not if we have to climb that ladder. If we're near the entrance, at least there's a chance someone will hear us if they're outside looking for us."

"Let's go a little ways further. At least until we know we've hit a dead end." I could see my words hadn't helped much. "Look, I know you're scared, but we'll be okay. You just have to keep believing there's a way out."

"And if there isn't?"

"Think about it this way. The average person can go three minutes without air, three days without water, and three weeks without food."

"And then?"

I refused to say what we were both thinking.

"Nick, there's something I need to tell you in case …"

She took a deep breath, cupped her hand over mine, and clicked off the light. The darkness suffocated us.

She squeezed my hand and said in a husky voice, "I have to tell you something. It's about this bruise on my forehead."

With each word, her heated breath blew against my skin. I wanted to pivot and tilt my head toward hers, but I refused. I'd watched too many television episodes where the killer manipulated the detective into believing she was innocent, and I was determined not to be tricked by Annie.

"Yes?"

"I lied when I told you yesterday that I'd fallen from my horse."

No kidding! Every time I turn around you're showing up. In the graveyard. On the train. Here.

The softness of her thumb stroking my knuckles began to distract me. *Oh, you're good. You're smooth as bat wings.* She rested her head against my chest, and I noticed a change in her breathing.

Here's the thing about girls: you can't trust them. At least, not when they want something from you. Guys melt when a girl snuggles up and gets all soft and gushy. At least I do. But that's mostly because as a boy with hairless armpits and glasses, I have no hope at all of penetrating the inner sanctuary of the pretty and popular girls group at my school.

I felt her breath on my cheek and knew even without the light that she was standing on her tiptoes. Swallowing, I said in a raspy voice, "So what did happen to you yesterday?"

"It was dark. I got to the stable a little after one a.m. You had left the saddle on my horse. That was fine. I hadn't asked you to remove it. Not that you would have even known how to undo the buckles and slide it off, anyway."

I couldn't be sure, but it felt like she was trying to hook her foot around my leg and pull me closer. Then again, maybe she was just trying to get her balance in the dark.

I said, "Go on."

"I walked my horse out of the stall, placed my foot in the stirrup, and had just swung my leg over when someone clubbed me from behind. Here, feel."

She took my hand and guided my fingers over her face until I felt the bump beneath her hair. Not much of a lump, but enough. I caught myself thinking: *Well, sure. And you could have just as easily slammed your head backwards into a beam on purpose in the hopes I would believe you.*

That's when I realized she was right about me. I *was* a hopeless cynic. I didn't trust anyone, certainly not those I suspected of murder.

But I also knew from all the cases I'd studied, watched on TV, and catagloged in the Cybersleuth database that it would be nearly impossible for a person Annie's age to kill someone and remain this composed. Impossible, that is, unless she was a professional actress—which she was.

"Who did you see in Boot Hill, Annie? Give me a name."

"I'm pretty sure that it was…"

The husky rattling sound of a rattlesnake's quivering shell silenced both of us.

I carefully untangled us, though I didn't dare move my feet.

Not an inch. I could tell from the way the beads shook that it was close. Maybe right next to us.

This is what I'd learned about rattlesnakes: they're deadly.

After my afternoon chat with Deputy Garrett, I'd decided to stop by the general store and see what I could learn about the native wildlife of Deadwood. The book on brown bears and other indigenous mammals had proved to be a very interesting read. The book was the last thing I'd read before dropping off to sleep. That was how I'd known about the musky scent of the brown bear and how bats congregated in caves during the winter to hibernate. The book on snakes, and rattlesnakes in particular, had intrigued me. For instance, I didn't know that they could detect movement from as far away as forty feet. Or that even in darkness they could strike with deadly accuracy.

I imagined the snake's body coiled at my feet, its tongue tasting the air and sensing the increased heat of my skin as adrenaline coursed through my body. Like a spring tensioned down until it's ready to snap, the snake would be poised and ready to sink its fangs into my flesh. A single bite and within minutes my muscles would begin to die. Capillaries and veins would expand and burst, causing my leg to swell and turn black. The book had warned that death from snakebite, though rare, was excruciatingly painful.

I felt Annie reach her arm around my waist and probe the waistband of my jeans until she found the hilt of the Schofield. Slowly, she eased the revolver out.

Darkness amplified her thumb clicking the hammer into place.

The agitated shaking of the snake's rattler intensified.

I flicked on my Streamlight and aimed it downward. The gun erupted, and the snake blasted into a bloody pink pulp. The shot, coming so close, made it almost impossible to hear anything other than the sharp ringing in my ears, but I heard myself shouting: "BLANKS? ISN'T THAT WHAT YOU SAID? THAT THESE GUNS ONLY FIRED BLANKS!"

Annie eyed the revolver with a sheepish grin. *Where there's one there could be others*, I thought, spraying the beam over the floor.

Stepping over the snake, I eased toward the unexplored tunnel.

She pulled me back. "Don't," she said.

"SNAKE GOT IN HERE SOMEHOW AND WE'RE A LONG WAY FROM THE MAIN ENTRANCE. I'M BETTING THAT'S OUR WAY OUT."

I suppose she saw the logic in my comment because she thumbed the hammer and aimed the gun at the floor in front of us.

We entered the last tunnel, moving slowly in single file. The shaft led us deeper into the mine along a meandering route bracketed every twenty feet or so with support beams. I saw evidence of gouging in the walls, as though someone had hacked away at the rock in an attempt to find gold. Cracks dissected the walls. *Easily wide enough for a snake to crawl in.* We reached a sharp bend, turned the corner, and stopped abruptly when my gaze fell upon a claw of curled fingers.

Jesse James lay facedown, one arm outstretched, a marble-eye staring blankly at my feet. His other arm, now brownish-black, rested under his chin, making it look as if he were napping. The bulge of meat below his chin and around his swollen neck had turned purple from where blood pooled up beneath the skin. No mistaking the cause of death. Puncture wounds on his neck indicated a rattler's deadly bite. *Just as I suspected*.

I smiled. Not so Annie could see, of course. She still stood behind me holding the Schofield. But the gun, the second victim, and her expert kill of the snake all proved I'd been right about my hunch. I *knew* who the killer was. All that remained was to escape the mine before I died.

I felt Annie tapping my shoulder. I looked back and saw her speaking to me.

"Huh?" I said.

"I FEAR PEOPLE SELLING!"

"Yeah, Mom does too. She hates it when salespeople come to our door selling stuff."

"NOT SELLING. YELLING. I HEAR PEOPLE YELLING!"

"Oh."

Annie spun and raced back to the entrance. I took a final look at James and followed.

CHAPTER SEVENTEEN
A WEAPON AND WEEPING AND GNASHING OF TEETH

The marshal looked at me as if *he'd* seen a ghost when we finally arrived back at the main entrance. He and several other men, Dad included, stood in the main staging area. They had burrowed through the rubble and now stood holding large, bulky flashlights aimed at us. I could tell Dad was mad. Everyone was.

"Young man, do you have any idea how much trouble you're in?" Dad asked.

Dad never called me "young man" unless he meant business. I nodded lamely. Apparently they'd been digging for some time. Had probably started right after I'd sprinted back to rejoin Annie. Without a word, Buckleberry took the gun from Annie.

"Outside!" he barked, pointing toward the trough carved from the rubble of fallen rock.

No need to tell Annie. She was already crawling toward the light, pawing at the rubble on all fours like a crazed animal desperate to escape its burrow. I followed with more self-control, feeling both ashamed and excited at once. Sure, we'd been trapped and could've died, but we hadn't. Besides, parents are always getting worked up about their kids when they get into trouble. Most times it's not a big deal.

But this *was* a big deal. We'd found the murder weapon and the killer's second victim.

Once I was outside in the morning sunshine, I brushed off my jeans and hurried over to Annie. She fell against me, sobbing hysterically. The sight of her friend Jess, dead, had shaken her.

The eye records images with great clarity. Sometimes we think it doesn't. Sometimes we think because we forget how someone looks after that person is gone that we weren't paying attention. That if we'd taken more time to study that person we could recall his or her face. I used to feel that way about my grandfather. I felt guilty that I couldn't remember how he looked. But in a dream once I saw him so clearly that the image of him fishing with me stayed for days. It was really weird because the two of us never went fishing. At least not that I could recall. But in my dream he wore a brown plaid shirt, old khakis with fish gut stains on them, and a floppy Gilligan hat with fishing lures hooked to the fabric. The only thing I could figure was that my eye had recorded all the times I'd seen granddad in that shirt and his garage work pants and that hat he wore when he cut grass, and I'd pulled it all together into a new memory that never happened.

This was my fear for Annie. That the scene of Dallas Joshua James lying dead in that cave would haunt her for years to come.

She made strange little wheezing sobs interspersed with hiccups and sniffles and pressed her fists against her bloodshot eyes.

I had the good sense to move her away from the mine and toward a fleet of waiting ATVs.

For a few moments I thought she was finished. Then she hurled herself around as if to run back to the cave. I wrapped my arms tightly around her until the flapping and convulsions stopped. Dad and Buckleberry emerged from the mine at the same time. I gently shoved Annie toward her uncle. She hurried toward him on unsteady legs, but her crying wasn't as extreme, and I began to think she might be okay.

Me, I wasn't sure about.

I asked Dad about my pony. He told me another staff member had already taken it back to town. He motioned to an ATV and we hopped on. I hugged his waist and we raced back to town. The excitement I'd felt in solving the murder faded and a sense of shame took its place. This was just the sort of thing Mom and Dad hated—me going off on my own without telling anyone.

After our bouncing, bumpy ride back to town, Dad explained that I was grounded until further notice. I didn't have to ask why, but he told me anyway. "You left the bunkhouse without telling anyone where you were going, borrowed a pony without permission (*not true, but I gathered the staff*

member was covering his tracks), went into a closed mine—
which is trespassing, and scared your mother half to death.
If the man at the corral hadn't mentioned that he'd seen you
riding toward the hills we might never have found you."

"But Dad," I protested. "Don't you want to know about
w—?"

"No! I want you to get in that office and do exactly as the
marshal says, do you understand me?"

I nodded and entered the marshal's trailer. Without looking
up, Buckleberry pointed to a chair and I sat. If he'd told me to
face the wall and put my nose on a chalkboard I wouldn't have
been surprised. I did exactly as Dad instructed and sat quietly,
even though I wanted to tell the marshal about the condition
of James's body and how we found the gun in the glory hole
and Annie's deadly aim at the snake. I wanted to tell him that
the sooner he called the county coroner, the faster we'd know
the time of death, that if he would go ahead and send the
Schofield off to ballistics, they would give him an answer as to
whether the slug in the barn matched the gun.

But I didn't say any of this because even I understood how
much trouble I was in this time. Or at least I *thought* I knew.

Still ignoring me, he punched a number into the phone
and waited.

When the emergency operator answered, Buckleberry
stated his name and location and announced that a body had
been found in an abandoned mine. The operator transferred
the call. I remained tight-lipped, listening while the marshal
repeated the information.

He hung up and turned his attention to me. His long, dull face sagged with the weight of weariness.

"They're sending someone out," he said stiffly. "Told me to stay put until they arrive. You know what this means, don't you? Deadwood Canyon becomes a crime scene. At least until they can confirm the death was an accident. All guests will be confined to their quarters until further notice. That means you, especially."

I sank into the chair. "I don't know what to say, Marshal. I was just following a lead."

He squeezed his eyes shut. For the first time I noticed his thinning gray hair and the brown splotches on the backs of his hands. The weight of trying to eke out a living in a tourist ghost town made him look tired and old. For a moment I felt sorry for him. This *was* my fault. He had deputized me, after all—even if it was all for fun and show.

He clenched his jaw and stared at me. "You and your leads," he said, rubbing the back of his neck. "I should've never agreed to any of this. Guess this is what happens when a man is desperate. And I am. Your dad was pretty insistent. He didn't come right out and say it, but I could see he was thinking of turning around and leaving. I don't know if he would have or not, but if you had complained too much, your family might have cut the vacation short. It's hard to refund money that's already spent." Resting his arms on the desk, he sighed. "So tell me. How far up your list of suspects was James? I would think pretty high."

"Are you really asking?"

"Not really."

There was something else I wanted to tell him, something even more important than finding the gun and the body. But I couldn't. Not yet, at least.

I said, "He didn't kill Billy the Kid. But I have evidence showing who did."

He looked amused. "Like the gun?" He took a quick peek at the revolver resting on the corner of his desk. He was about to say something more when Deputy Garrett knocked and entered. The deputy wore pressed gray slacks, a blue button-down collared shirt, and polished brown loafers. Without his customary rawhide lawman outfit, he could have passed for the sales assistant who'd waited on me the last time I'd upgraded my wireless plan.

"Lab just phoned me back with the ballistics report on that slug we pulled from the barn," Garrett declared.

Buckleberry looked irritated. "And?"

"Came from a Smith & Wesson .44 caliber Schofield."

"Like this one here on the desk?"

"Exactly like that one, boss."

The marshal smiled. The first genuine expression of relief I'd seen since we'd arrived. "Well, Deputy Caden, looks like you finally found something of interest. Of course all this proves is that someone used the Schofield for target practice up in the hayloft." Buckleberry said to Garrett, "Ride up to the mine and make sure no one goes in or out until the county coroner arrives. I don't want anybody else sneaking in and getting lost."

"But, boss. Today's my day off and I was going t—"

"Would you just get on up there? And don't forget to turn

on your handheld. Had some trouble here in the office last night …"

The marshal paused and, fixing his stare on me, said pointedly "… and couldn't reach you."

"Sure thing," the deputy grumbled, pulling the door shut behind him.

The marshal waited until Garrett left before adding, "As soon as the county coroner rules James's death an accident and their little investigation team clears out, I want you and your family to pack up and leave."

The blood drained from my face. "You can't kick us out. I didn't do anything wrong."

"Mine is off-limits. Has been for a while. You probably saw the closed sign and figured it didn't apply to you."

"The sign was tossed on top of some lumber. But *I* wasn't the one who took it down."

He hunched toward me, his face so bunched his eyes looked like tiny dots. "I've been in Deadwood nearly twenty years. Besides that snake bit, worst trouble we've ever had was a few broken bones and an occasional case of food poisoning. Then you show up and it's like a black cloud settles over the place. I'm not one to believe in ghosts and witches and curses but I swear, I think you must've put some kind of jinx on this town. Now, you want to tell your folks about the curfew or should I?"

I told Buckleberry I'd take care of it. And I did. Or I should say, Mom took care of me.

"YOU DID WHAT?"

Mom and Wendy sat around a campfire beside Cookie's Chuck Wagon Grill. Twenty or so other guests milled about in the open field, munching on ham biscuits, eggs, and fried bacon. The coolness of the morning melted under the heat of the blaze. Iron skillets hissed and popped with the sound of frying bacon.

"I thought Dad told you about the mine and the body I found," I replied, dropping onto a log bench carved to look like a beaver's tail.

"I haven't seen your father since he left to find you. That was over an hour ago. Where'd you go? And why didn't you tell someone you were leaving?"

I recounted my adventure in the mine and how the entrance caved in right after Annie arrived; how for a while we wandered around in the mine looking for another way out. "But only for a little while," I explained, trying to sound like getting trapped in an abandoned mine was no big deal. "You eating that?" I said to Wendy, reaching for a slice of bacon.

My sister smacked my hand.

"That's it! You're grounded!" Mom announced.

"I know. Dad already told me. At least you two can agree on something."

"Don't get smart with me, young man. You could've been killed."

I thought about mentioning the snake but decided not to.

"Really, Mom. It wasn't as scary as it sounds. I mean finding Jesse James's dead body sort of freaked me out, but then I—"

"WHAT?"

"Oh, did I forget to mention that? Yeah, Billy the Kid's killer struck again."

"I thought you told me he died of a snakebite," Dad remarked, walking up behind me.

Mom glared at Dad. "Frank, why didn't you tell me he'd found a dead person?"

"Because I knew as soon as I did, you'd blame me."

Mom scowled at Dad. "What's that supposed to mean?"

"Just that every time Nick does something dumb you act like it's my fault."

"Mom, Dad used the D word."

"Sorry, honey. Your father didn't mean to, did you Frank?"

"No, honey. Daddy didn't really mean to call your brother stupid."

Wendy thrust out her palm. "A dollar. Just like you promised."

Dad ruffled through his wallet and gave Wendy a crisp bill. For the past few months, our family had been on a kick to cut down on the sarcasm and negative talk. Calling someone dumb, stupid, or an idiot cost you a dollar. I was already deeply in debt to Wendy. She had a whole jar full of IOUs from me.

Mom returned to *her* carping, which, according to the rules, was okay. "My point is, Frank, Nick isn't the only one who has a tendency to leave without first telling someone where he's going."

"You're not going to bring up that fishing trip again, are you? How many times do I have to tell you? My cell died."

"You could have borrowed a phone, couldn't you?"

Wendy scooted over and, shutting out my mom and dad's arguing, asked, "Did you really find another body?"

"Give me your bacon and I'll tell you all about it."

"Get your own."

I eyed the line at the chuck wagon and decided I just wasn't that hungry.

"You didn't answer me when I asked about the snake bite," said Dad, taking a seat on the other bench.

I waited until Wendy looked back toward the herd of buffalo before snatching her bacon. "Oh, that," I said, chewing. "The snake killed him but only in the same way a bullet killed Billy the Kid, I'm sure of it."

Mom, I guess sensing that Dad had tuned her out, turned her attention back to me. "You're in serious trouble."

Dad, trying to sound like he was in charge, piped up. "I already told him he was grounded."

Wendy swiveled and eyed her plate. "Nick! I told you no! Dad! Did you see what he did?"

"We all are," I announced.

"All are what?" asked Dad.

"Grounded. Everyone."

Mom slumped onto the bench next to Dad. "I don't understand, Nick."

I flipped my bangs back and sighed. "The marshal called the coroner and was told that as of right now, Deadwood is a crime scene. All of it. No one can leave their room."

Wendy went ballistic. "But that's not fair! *I* didn't do anything wrong. Nick's the one who should be punished, not me."

"I know," said Dad. "But if the marshal says for us to stay put, we don't have any choice."

"Can't he put Nick in jail instead?"

Dad, looking exasperated, shook his head. I saw the other guests beginning to look in our direction. Apparently word was beginning to leak that a body had been found and I was the one who'd discovered it—and got everyone banished to their rooms.

"Can I still go to the Prairie Dog Poetry reading?" my sister whined. "It starts at nine."

"If Nick says the marshal wants us in the bunkhouse, then that means you too, honey."

"This is so unfair!"

"Maybe later, honey. After all this blows over. But right now," he paused and surveyed the crowd staring at us, "the less we're seen the better."

I should've told them about us getting booted out of town right then but I just couldn't. Everyone was so bummed, me included.

"Nick, go to your room and stay there," said Dad. "I don't even want to hear that you were on the porch, understood?"

Wendy, sounding like her usual sarcastic self, added, "Yeah, Nick. Why don't you play detective in your room?"

I looked to my mother for moral support, but she only came to my defense long enough to lob her own verbal jab. In a sad and tired-sounding voice she said, "That's enough, Wendy. I'm sure Nick feels bad about all the trouble he's caused for us and everyone else, isn't that right?"

BUT I HAVEN'T DONE ANYTHING WRONG! I wanted to scream. *I didn't cause the tunnel to collapse. I didn't put Earp's gun in the mine. And I certainly didn't make that snake bite Jesse*

James, who, by the way, shouldn't have been in the mine in the first place. Of course I said none of this, just chewed on my bottom lip while staring at my sneakers. I had a pretty good idea who the real killer was. Finding James dead in the mine and the gun in the glory hole confirmed my hunch. All I needed was the chance to prove it—a chance that now looked hopelessly lost since I couldn't leave my room.

Wendy tossed the remains of her breakfast into the fire and glowered at me. Mom looked as if she were about to say something, but just then the marshal rode up on an ATV.

"Nick told us about the curfew, Marshal. We were just about to head back to the bunkhouse. Any idea how long we'll be confined to our rooms?"

"He didn't say anything about the other thing?"

"There's more?" Mom asked.

"Yes, ma'am, I'm afraid so. Mr. Caden, remember the other day when you came to me and asked if I'd let your son play detective, and you promised there wouldn't be any trouble? Remember that?" Dad nodded. "Now I got a dead actor in a mine that's supposed to be off limits and a whole lot of questions from the county deputy that I can't answer. I told your son that I was sending you home, but I guess he didn't relay that part of the message. I think that's best for everyone involved. I was all set to refund the balance of your money, but I can't. At least not yet."

Dad cut his eyes my direction but didn't say anything. "So we're being evicted?"

"Something like that." The marshal folded his arms. "I could charge Nick with trespassing. He knew the mine was off-limits, even if the sign wasn't at the entrance so he could see it." Shifting his gaze toward me he said, "But I won't. For now."

"Marshal, if you'll just listen," I interrupted. "I can tell you who the killer is and we can clear all this up."

"First off, I wouldn't believe anything you tell me right now. You promised you'd obey the rules and you haven't. Second, I'm not about to arrest someone just because *you* think he or she killed someone. Watching TV and figuring out who done it ... that's the dumbest thing I've ever heard."

"Marshal, unless there's something more, we'll head on back to our bunkhouse now."

"You do that. All except him." The marshal pointed his finger at me. "You, come with me. The county coroner wants to ask you a few questions."

"Oh, great. I have to miss the Prairie Dog Poetry reading but he still gets to play supersleuth?" Wendy said. "This is so not right."

"I know, Wendy. But there will be other opportunities."

"Not here there won't, Mom. We're never coming back to this place. You and Dad know it."

"Tell you what," the marshal volunteered. "Let me make a few phone calls; see what else is going on in the area. I can recommend a couple of nice motels. Maybe you can take in some of the other sights in the area on your way back to the interstate."

"Whatever," Wendy said bitterly and stormed off.

The marshal jabbed his thumb toward his idling ATV. "Come on. Let's get this over with so you and your family can hit the road."

CHAPTER EIGHTEEN
HIGH MARKS FOR MURDER

The marshal led me through the small cluster of photojournalists snapping pictures of the mine. Deputy Garrett stood with his arms crossed guarding the entrance while a crew of county workers carefully removed the rubble and reinforced the opening with temporary pillars.

"If law enforcement personnel scanned the emergency frequencies like these reporters do, we'd catch a lot more criminals." Buckleberry lifted the yellow crime scene tape. I ducked under and paused, waiting for him. "I'll stay out here. Not big on small places. Took every ounce of courage I had to crawl in to find you. Hurry, now. Don't want this thing to drag out any longer than it has to."

I followed the incandescent glow of stick lights, returning to where I'd found the body earlier that morning. A county deputy met me near the place where Annie had killed the snake. Further on, a heavy-set, gray-haired woman knelt over James. She wore a baggy navy blue jumpsuit and teal footies over her shoes. She jabbed a temperature probe into James's skin and pressed it downward.

"You the one who found the body?" the deputy asked in a dull voice.

"Yes."

"What can you tell me?"

I explained that I'd been informed by one of the staff at Deadwood that another employee was thought to be drinking on the job and how, if I could verify the allegation, that individual might have a reason to see Billy the Kid dead.

The officer looked confused.

"Long story," I added. "Billy was one of the characters in town. I believe the actor who played the role of Billy the Kid has been murdered."

That drew a surprised reaction from the deputy. He pointed to the body. "That the way you found him?"

I said it was.

"Got a time of death, Janice?"

"Best guess is between eight and twelve hours ago. Won't be able to say with certainty until we get the body back to the lab."

"What time did you say you arrived here?" I heard the deputy ask.

"Around daybreak. I woke up at five, got my pony, and rode up, *rode* being a generous term for her speed. If I had to guess, I would say I got here a little before six."

"Alone?"

I told him how Annie surprised me about the time I found the gun. "Right after that the shaft collapsed and we came back this way looking for an air vent."

"Janice, you find anything on the body to change your opinion as to the cause of death?"

The coroner replied, "It would appear this poor man was the victim of a rattlesnake bite. And a nasty one at that. See here?" With the tip of a pencil she touched two puncture wounds. "Straight into his jugular vein. Once the venom entered his bloodstream the toxins would have attacked his nervous system, causing neurotoxicity, making breathing difficult. Most likely he died of respiratory failure within minutes."

"But if it was a snakebite, wouldn't you expect to see fang marks on his calf or ankle?" I pointed out.

"Might have been on his knees," the deputy replied irritably. "Looking for something. Who knows what?"

"Just before we found the body, Annie shot a large rattlesnake. Any way to test the venom to see if it matches what's in his body?" I asked.

"Why certainly, if we had the snake," said the coroner.

I glanced around. No trace of the snake.

The coroner shrugged. "Perhaps a rodent carried if off. I find it odd, however, that there would be a rattlesnake this far from the entrance. They feed on bugs and rodents. I would expect to find them nearer to their food source."

I told them about finding bats down the other shaft and suggested maybe a bat had carried away the carcass.

"So, Janice," the deputy was saying. "Can we rule his death an accident?"

"I would say yes if not for this." With her fingers, the coroner parted the hair on the back of James's head. "Appears to be a contusion just above the base of his skull. What you say is true. The bites are in an unusual location. It's possible our victim may have been unconscious when he was bitten."

"But wouldn't that suggest he was ..."

"Murdered? Indeed it would."

"Then if you don't mind," I said, my voice quivering with excitement, "I'd like you to examine another corpse."

"Oh? Is it nearby?"

"Yes, ma'am. In the graveyard on Boot Hill."

CHAPTER NINETEEN
BODY OF EVIDENCE

I sat in the rear of a rickety buckboard, my legs dangling off the back. Behind me Marshal Buckleberry led a convoy of reporters, the county deputy, Deputy Garrett, the coroner, my parents, and Wendy out of town and toward Boot Hill. At first the marshal had bristled at the presence of the media, but he must've seen the value of the exposure because he allowed them to tag along. I suppose even a rumor of a murder was better than tumbleweeds blowing down Main Street.

We reached the trail leading up to the cemetery, and I hopped down and followed the others up the twisting path. The cold front had blown the sky clear of clouds, leaving a brilliant blue tarp overhead, but the wind had a definite bite. I wished I'd worn something more than my lightweight jacket.

Brushing bangs from my eyes, I peeked back and saw Annie trudging up the path. I couldn't tell if it was intentional or not, but she seemed to be avoiding me. I suspected part of Annie's odd behavior had something to do with the death of her friend, Jess. But I also wondered if she might be dreading the trip back to Boot Hill. She still had not revealed the identity of the man we'd seen in the graveyard, and it got me wondering: *Does she know that I know who the killer is? Is that why she won't look at me?*

We reached a short plateau offering a good resting place and paused to let the others catch up. When I saw Annie glace over, I gave her a reassuring wink. You know, just to gauge her reaction. Her eyes found mine and became as cold as the snowy crust capping those Rocky Mountain peaks.

Here's the thing you need to know about murder: killing is never as sterile and impersonal as the movies and television make it out to be. Only a heartless monster can kill and not be affected by the act of taking a life. And even then, they are changed and driven deeper into the dark world. That's what guilt does; it buries you. I know this because in addition to watching lots of television crime shows and figuring out "who done it," I also examine the "why they done it." The *why* is way more interesting than the *who*.

Given the right circumstances, any of us can be taught to kill. The question is, will we?

I remember one time finding a mound of ants in our backyard and stomping that conical hill until there was nothing but black specks in the dirt. We swat mosquitoes and think nothing of it. Kill roaches and wasps and set traps for mice. When I was in the fourth grade, Tommy Brewer dared me to shove a lit firecracker into the mouth of a frog. My point is, any of us can change and become a murderer when placed in the right circumstances.

Sweet Annie, good-natured and wholesome Annie—the girl who'd met me outside the saloon and tried to teach me how to fire a revolver, the dead-eye killer of rattlesnakes, and the haunting shadow that magically appears around every turn—that Annie had changed. And not in a good way.

We reached the graveyard, and the crowd fanned out.

The marshal took a position beneath the gnarled tree and scowled at me. "Well? Which grave is it?"

"In a minute, Marshal. There are a few things I'd like to say first."

My sister slapped a hand to her forehead. "Oh pleeeeease!"

"I want to thank my friend Annie for sticking by me. No matter how much trouble I got in this week, she was always there beside me. Sometimes before I even knew she was there."

Her cheeks reddened and she tried to shrink back in the crowd, but there was only so much room along the edge of the cemetery.

"I'm due at a hearing this afternoon," the county deputy piped up. "Is this going to take much longer?"

"Before we exhume the body of Billy the Kid, I want to assure you that even though the murderer is among us, we are safe."

A murmur rumbled through the crowd. Annie cocked her head like she wasn't sure if she'd heard me right.

"Last night when I returned to my room, I got to thinking that this is a murder investigation. And yes, that's exactly what it is: a homicide. I thought back to several television episodes I'd seen, most dealing with events similar to what happened in Lazy Jack's stable two days ago."

"Hey, Nick, if I'm not the killer, can I go?" Wendy shouted at me.

"Actually, sis, believe it or not, you helped me. If you hadn't insisted there were such things as ghosts, I might never have found the killer. Or found those Bible references. Thanks, by the way, to whoever left that Gideon Bible in my room."

I saw the county deputy look over at the coroner and tap his watch.

"So, yes, Wendy. Because of your infatuation with the occult and gothic myths, I was able to solve the case."

"Actually, you haven't," Marshal Buckleberry said impatiently. "You still haven't produced one shred of evidence that there has even been a murder."

"I have Billy the Kid's body, that's a start."

"No you don't," Annie shot back. "*You* don't even know where it is."

She was right. I honestly didn't know. I wished now I'd paid closer attention to where the mysterious stranger dug the grave, but at the time I'd thought it would be easy to find.

"We're leaving," said the county deputy, motioning to the coroner to gather her things.

"How 'bout this one?" said Pat Garrett. He'd changed into his lawman outfit. With the toe of his cowboy boot he poked at a swatch of matted grass.

"I … don't know," I replied. "That *could* be the right one."

He knelt and pointed to the grass. "Right there, see? You can just make out the muddy discoloring like maybe someone's been digging."

"I can't say for sure. Was pretty dark. I was standing over there, behind those rocks. I didn't get a great look."

Buckleberry motioned to the undertaker, a string bean of a man dressed in black. No doubt the undertaker was there purely for visual effect. I couldn't wait for the photographers to snap a picture of the undertaker standing over Billy's corpse. *Will probably make the front page of the Denver paper.*

I left the digging to the worker bees and drifted back to join my family.

"Nick, I don't know what you hope to accomplish with this little stunt, but mark my words, there will be consequences," Dad said with his usual sternness. "That business in the mine was bad enough, but this? Making everyone stand around while you hunt for a corpse in a graveyard?"

"Trust me, Dad, I know what I'm doing. I only wish I'd gone to the marshal last night as soon as I figured out who the killer was. If I had, Jesse James might still be alive."

"You don't get it, do you, Nick?" my sister said. "The only reason the marshal let you come up here is because he's hoping you'll look like an idiot—which the rest of us know you are."

"That's enough, Wendy," Mom said halfheartedly.

Wendy kept on. "Those reporters over there? They can't wait to write about how some teen with a wild imagination led the marshal of Deadwood on a manhunt for a killer who's been dead for more than a century. I knew you'd mess up our vacation. You always do."

I waited for Mom to add her pithy comment about how I'd ruined her vacation too, but this time she kept quiet. I think she genuinely felt sorry for me. But she didn't need to. I knew what I was doing. At least I thought I did.

"Hey, I think we found something," Garrett called out.

"Now you'll see I'm right," I said smugly.

"And if you're not?" Mom demanded. "If it turns out this was all a colossal waste of time? Then mark my words: you're online cybersleuthing, virtual detective gaming days are over."

"You can't do that. I'm vice president of our club. And next year, when Bart McLean doesn't run for re-election, I might be even be president."

"Not only *can* I, but I will. That," said Mom, eyeing the partially uncovered grave, "is the direct result of your obsession with video gaming and all those detective shows. Don't you see, Nick? You've turned our vacation *into* one of your cybersleuth games."

"Mom's right, son. You need to spend less time on online cybersleuthing and more time playing sports. Maybe it's not too late to get you into a summer baseball league or maybe sign you up for soccer."

"But I hate team sports."

"All the more reason to get you involved," Mom said.

Shoving my hands in my pockets, I turned my attention back toward the headstones.

The previous day's rain had softened the ground, making the undertaker's job easy. He and Deputy Garrett gouged the earth with shovels, piling up uneven chunks of grass and dirt. The growing mound became a small monument to Billy the

Kid. I wondered how the young man would be remembered. Cowboy and actor? Son and friend? A blazing star rocketing toward the bright lights of Hollywood only to be blasted out of the sky by a jealous coworker? I wondered too how long he'd suffered in that hayloft before I arrived; how many gurgling breaths he'd taken before his eyes fixed on the ceiling and he saw the white light—or the dark, wispy shapes of demons rushing to sweep him away. Maybe he'd died quickly. Maybe he hadn't had time to feel the terrifying fear that precedes death. But I had my doubts. I'd seen the shock in his eyes and the blood on his hands. He had tried for a few seconds—or minutes—to plug the geyser spewing blood from his chest.

And had failed.

Garrett and the undertaker tossed the shovels aside. The two of them reached down and, taking the two ends, lifted the long sheath of black plastic from the grave. The thin polymer did little to keep the pungent stench of decay from escaping. Gagging, the undertaker went trotting over to the edge of the cemetery and threw up. Garrett clamped his hand over his mouth and nose and turned away.

"Well, son. Could be you were right," said the marshal. "Looks like we do have a fresh body. Deputy, cut that plastic and let's take a look."

Pat Garrett tucked his nose inside his shirt and inhaled deeply. Then taking a knife from his pocket, he dropped to one knee and cut the plastic. Instantly flies swarmed, their buzzing adding to the grotesque sight of the victim's sunken face. The shotgun blast had caved in one half of the skull leaving a large corroded cavity of dried blood, bone fragments, and black fur.

One opal eye looked out. I stepped closer, noting the small brown bear's sneering grin under its curled lips.

My stomach churned, and I whirled and jogged back toward the path upwind of the smell.

"That's your vic?" I heard the marshal saying. "You drag us all the way up here for that? A dead bear? Deputy, hurry and throw some dirt on that poor creature before we all start puking."

The crowd did not need to be told to leave. The exodus began with Wendy at the head of the stampede. I remained bent forward with my hands on my knees, taking in large gulps of air. Out of the corner of my eye I noticed Annie looking at me with a strange, sad expression as if to say, "I told you so."

Told me what? That it was all a joke? That the prank was at my expense? She followed her uncle back down the trail, leaving me with the deputy and the dead bear.

I heard the clank of shovels banging together and knew the deputy was finished burying the bear. I looked across the valley for a long while, savoring its rustic beauty. I'd guessed right about the identity of the killer—even if I hadn't been able to prove it. Even if I didn't have a body. At least I could take satisfaction in that.

Wyatt Earp ambled over. "Guess we'd better get going," he drawled. "Marshal wants me to escort you back to the bunk-house. And I know it looks bad, you not finding a body and all, but don't let it get to you. I know what it's like to have people saying things about you that aren't true. Know what I mean?" He paused, allowing his words to sink in.

I thought of how eager I'd been to tell Annie about Earp's alleged drinking problem and felt ashamed. I'd never seen him drinking, only heard the rumor. But I'd latched onto it because it fit what I wanted to believe about the investigation.

"If you can't say something nice about a man, then keep your mouth shut. That's what my Marge always said."

"Sounds like your wife was a smart woman."

"You have no idea, son. Look here, finding the truth is never easy. Anyone who says otherwise doesn't know what he's talking about. Fact is, those lies we believe about ourselves are the *real* ghosts that haunt us. The 'what ifs' and 'wish I hadn'ts' and 'I'm not good enoughs.' Those whispering voices that tear us down and leave us feeling worthless and ugly. It's those spooks you need to be worried about. You get what I'm saying?"

I did. But I wasn't doubting myself. At least, not regarding the case. I knew what I'd seen.

"I'm not upset about this," I said, falling in step with Mr. Earp as we angled toward the trail. "I mean, I hate that everyone had to see that back there. But there's no doubt Bill was killed in Lazy Jack's with your gun. And now I know for sure who murdered him."

"So you still think Bill is dead and *not* on his way back from L.A. like the marshal says?"

"I don't think it. I know it. And if I hurry, I can prove who the killer is before the county deputy and coroner leave. But I'll need your help."

"Can't let you into the marshal's office, if that's what you're going to ask."

"Actually, it's a lot more complicated than that. And dangerous." *Especially for me.*

Smiling, Mr. Earp asked, "How do you know I'm not the killer?"

"Who says you're not? And if you are, this is your chance to get rid of the one person who knows who the killer is. So, will you help me?"

"What do you have in mind?"

Taking a huge gamble, I told him my plan—at least the part I wanted him to know—and we started down the trail toward town.

CHAPTER TWENTY
FOOL'S GOLD

"**H**ey, I've been wondering what happened to you." Annie stood outside the blacksmith shop, acting all friendly as if nothing had happened on Boot Hill. Relief can make you giddy, and she certainly looked chipper.

With Earp's permission, I'd stopped by to tell her good-bye. It was part of my plan, the part I'd told him about. Motioning inside, we stepped into the shop and out of earshot of the workers by the O.K. Corral.

"Thanks for sticking by me up there in the graveyard," I replied, trying to sound disappointed.

Her mood instantly changed. "What'd you expect me to

do? Tell the world I'd seen a body buried up there too? You get to go home when this is over. I still have to work here."

"Did you put that note in my backpack?"

"No! How could you say such a thing? Of course not."

"Funny how I found it and then found you waiting for me at the bottom of Boot Hill that evening."

"I told you. Uncle Walt said for me to—"

"I know, I know. Keep an eye on me. Problem is, you've been keeping too close an eye on me. It seems you show up every time the killer does."

"You're not mad because I tried to help, are you?"

"Help? What help? You're like the fair-weather friend who splits when the teacher walks into the room and catches you peeking at her homework assignment."

"I let you into my uncle's office, didn't I?" she answered. "That little stunt almost cost me my job, thank you very much."

"I didn't twist your arm."

"No, you certainly did not. Maybe I should just go."

She pivoted to leave, and I caught her by the elbow. "Wait. I'm sorry. It's just that ..." I hesitated, studying her eyes. I needed to know how far I'd set the hook; how committed she was to keeping an eye on me.

"Your mom's right. You're obsessed with playing detective stuff."

"Could be she's right. It's all I think about. Even now I keep wondering if I could have solved this case sooner and maybe saved your friend Jess if I'd paid more attention to the evidence in front of me."

"Oh, give me a break. Haven't you heard anything my uncle has been saying? Billy's alive. Uncle Walt let me listen to the voice mail. He wanted me to know just how childish I was to let you drag me into this whole ghost murder mystery mess. Said it was time I stop acting like such a scatterbrained tomboy and grow up. He's thinking of sending me to an all-girl prep school."

"Too bad. Near as I can tell you're the only fun thing there is in this tumbleweed, dead-end town."

"Thanks," she said, half-smiling. "I think."

"Anyway, just came to say it's been fun and hope there's no hard feelings." I paused, glancing casually around the shop at the horseshoes and smelting equipment. "You never did finish telling me who pushed you and gave you that nasty bruise."

She looked down, pushed her hands in the back pockets of her jeans, and mumbled, "Oh, you know what? I changed my mind about that. After that business in the graveyard I realized I was wrong to even bring it up. Just forget I said anything."

"Okay," I said, trying to sound concerned. "But remember, Annie. Whoever did that to you is probably the same person who killed Billy the Kid and whacked your friend Jess in the back of the head."

"What are you talking about? Jess died of a snakebite."

"After he'd been knocked unconscious. Ask the coroner if you don't believe me. She discovered a knot on the back of his head. Looks like someone clubbed James, hauled him to the back of the mine, and somehow enticed that rattler to bite. Of course, I can't prove that any more than I can prove Bell was killed in the hayloft. But I just thought you should know if you *were* pushed, that someone is probably still around and willing to do anything to keep you quiet."

Looking flustered she said, "I, ah … thanks for the heads up." Standing on her tiptoes, she kissed me quickly on the cheek. "You be careful, Nick Caden."

Annie trotted away and I headed back to the corral to find Earp. I found him readying a pony for me. "Think she'll go for it?" he asked.

"No doubt. She's too scared not to."

He lifted the latch of the stall and led my pony out. Handing me the reins he said, "I hope you know what you're doing, son. You're taking a huge risk."

"Don't I know it. But I'll be fine. I have a little something I think will help me."

"Oh? And what's that?"

"Truth. I heard it can set you free. Now let's hope it can corral the bad guys too."

The crime scene tape remained stretched across the entrance to the mine. The excavated lumber, broken beam supports, rocks, and tools were piled just where Buckleberry and the others had left them. I knew I had one chance to catch the killer. One wrong move and I would vanish just like Billy the Kid, the farmer in the saloon, the comic cowboy on the Big Sky, and the bandit outside the bank. Poof … never to be heard from again. The ghosts in Deadwood weren't real; I knew that much. But I didn't need to see the evidence of wispy phantom figures to know that the killer was close by. I could sense it.

I ducked my head under the temporary pillars and listened. Nothing. Just the sound of my own anxious breathing. I checked to make sure the flashlight and other tools hadn't fallen out of my jacket pocket, then entered the killer's lair.

The darkness felt worse than before, the closeness of the walls suffocating. I reached the miners' staging area and took a few moments to slow my breathing. I didn't dare turn on the light. Not yet. Not until I had the snare set.

Onward I crept, counting my steps and trying to remember how far back we'd come before reaching the cave of bats. It seemed longer in the dark, and I had to tell myself I wasn't lost. Couldn't get lost. There was just the one long tunnel. As long as my feet kept tripping over the pushcart rails, I would be fine.

At last I reached the bats. Their clicking sounds served as the perfect cover, allowing me to bump my way along until I found the ladder. I checked my pockets once more. The last thing I needed was to drop my light and tools in the dark. Swinging one leg over, I felt for the rung, found good footing, and began my descent.

Around the fifth or sixth rung I detected a change in the bats clicking. Hurrying, I climbed down and reached the next level. Peering up into darkness, I strained to hear. Someone was definitely coming; the shuffle of feet confirmed it.

I moved quickly across the chamber, feeling my way along until I found the one tunnel. Scraping into walls with my elbows and thighs, I moved toward the place where I'd found James's body, waited until I was around the corner, and clicked on the flashlight. But only for a second. Only long enough to sweep the beam side-to-side and examine the length of the passageway. The twisting shaft went back much further than I'd expected. Behind me came a grunt of effort followed by the rough sound of the ladder shifting against the ledge. Breaking into a jog, I hurried away from my stalker.

The tunnel ended like all the others—a dead end.

I clicked on the light for a moment and found that what I'd thought was a wall of support beams was really a rough wooden door attached with three sturdy hinges. Timber posts had been cemented into the wall. Someone had gone to great effort to seal off this end of the tunnel, and I had a hunch I knew why. Light off.

I pushed against the door and felt it give a little. Using a Barlow knife I'd purchased at the general store, I felt for the crack between door and post, slipped the blade through, and lifted the J hook. The door opened and I stepped in, pushing it shut. Confident that I'd baited the trap properly, I turned on the light and aimed the beam at the glittering flecks of gold embedded in the ceiling and walls. Amber flecks glittered with such brilliance and density that the walls appeared to be moving. For several moments I stood transfixed by the sight. This wasn't just a glory hole. This was the mother lode.

"You should've left when you had the chance, boy."

Instantly a light blinded me.

The intensity of the spotlight consumed my flashlight's puny beam. Beyond the glare of the spotlight, I heard the sound of a magazine sliding into place and knew, even blinded, that there was a gun aimed at me.

"After the way you embarrassed yourself in the graveyard,

I felt sure you would be on your way home by now. Guess I misjudged you."

"You seem to be doing that a lot lately," I replied, struggling to keep my voice from cracking.

"Careful now with that knife. Wouldn't want you to get any ideas."

My hand froze. I'd hoped to tuck it away after entering the chamber, but I'd been so caught off guard by the brilliance of the gold flecks that I'd forgotten.

"Kick it over here. Excellent. Now the flashlight."

It, too, clanked onto the floor.

"Good. Now get those hands up where I can see them."

This was not exactly how I'd planned to confront the killer, but it could still work. I just needed to buy a little more time.

I lifted my right arm, but instead of raising it over my head I used my hand to shield my eyes. It knocked the glare down just enough for me to see past the miner's light. Annie stood near the light hunched forward, her head sagging, and bangs flopping into her face.

I said, "How you doing? Doing okay? Anything you need?"

"I, ah … I'm fine," she stammered.

She appeared to be on the verge of tears. I could see why. I'd have been terrified too if someone had a Glock 19 handgun pressed against the back of my head.

"You can't possibly think you'll get away with killing the two of us, deputy."

"Oh? And why not?"

Deputy Pat Garrett removed the miner's light from his forehead and propped it on the floor, angling it in such a way that it illuminated the room and cast more light on Annie. Her wrists were tied in front, ankles unbound.

"I figure right about now your parents will start wondering where you wandered off to, and they'll send out a search party. No doubt the marshal will ride up to the railroad trestle and find the spot where the two of you stood too close to the edge. He'll see where the ledge gave way and a bloodstain near the river's edge and assume the bodies were swept downstream. Be just another tragic accident in a long line that'll finally put this place out of business. So what is it exactly I'm not understanding?"

"That tunnel behind you," I said. "The one you and Annie came in through. If I follow it out it'll take me to the train trestle, right?"

"Every time." With his free hand, Garrett shoved Annie onto her knees and pressed the gun execution-style against her head. A look of panic swept across her face.

"Bill Bell found out about the gold in the mine, didn't he?" I said grimly. "Threatened to go to the marshal, and that's why you killed him."

"Caught me coming out of here a few days ago. He wanted to know what I was doing. Told him it was none of his business. He reminded me 'bout that kid getting bit and how the marshal warned us that we couldn't afford another mining disaster, that more bad press would shut us down. That was all I needed: that punk actor blabbing his mouth to Buckleberry."

"So you shot him."

He shrugged. "Could be your girl here shot him."

"For a little while I wondered if she had," I admitted, casually moving toward the knife. "But I couldn't find any reason for Annie to want Bell dead. I admit she has an uncanny ability of showing up at the wrong time. Why not just tell Bell what you found and cut him in on it?" I surveyed the walls again, taking in the abundance of gold. "From the looks of it, there's plenty to go around."

"Spend enough time studying people like I have and you become a pretty good judge of character. Get a gauge on how they'll react. Bill wasn't going to play nice. Sure I could've given him a cut, but I knew he'd want a bigger slice and would keep on threatening me until I gave him a larger share. Pretty soon it would've been me doing all the work and Bill living high. Just like it's always been for me. Wasn't going to be that way, not this time. Don't think about going for that knife, boy. You'll never make it."

I froze. I could feel my palms perspiring and nervous sweat trickling down my sides. Licking dry lips I said, "One question. Why put that note in my backpack?"

"You don't know? I thought you were the boy-wonder detective and knew everything. I needed to throw you off, make you think there was a body buried on Boot Hill. Otherwise you might have kept looking."

"So you shot a bear? Isn't that ... overkill?"

"That one's been getting after the cattle and scaring the horses. Was a nuisance. Like you. Marshal wanted me to trap it and let the wildlife folks haul it away. But when you showed up, I got another idea. Turns out a right good one too, judging from the reaction in the graveyard this morning."

"So when you came at us with the shovel the other night, that was just to scare us and get Annie to keep quiet."

"You wouldn't shut up about Bill being murdered. Kept the marshal all in a snit about that."

"So after you shot Bell and put his body in the trunk of the Charger …"

Garrett grunted.

"It's okay to say it, Deputy Garrett. Confession is good for the soul. Least that's what I hear."

"Thought you'd found Bill's body for sure," said Garrett, sidestepping my suggestion. "Especially when I heard you were poking around in the employee parking lot. Guess I caught a break there."

"Wish I'd figured it out sooner. I knew something in that car stank, but I didn't make the connection until I caught a whiff of that carcass this morning. I hadn't been absolutely sure it was you who killed Bell until you pointed out the fresh grave. Only you would have known where you buried that bear. And there wouldn't have been any reason to dig a fresh grave and throw me off your trail, like you said. Thanks for confirming what I already knew, Deputy."

"You don't know anything."

"Oh, but I do. You want to know how I know? Because I've seen the same scenario played out countless times on cop shows. The last was on *Over My Dead Body … and Beyond*. In that one a disgruntled employee at a mini-storage business finds several boxes of old letters in one of the units. He starts peeling off the stamps and selling them to collectors. When a coworker finds out, he threatens to tell the owner. After all, tampering with mail is a federal offense. The coworker ends up dead. Near the end of the show the body of a second worker is found—the one the lead investigator thought was the real thief. Took me a while to lay the facts of this case over all the shows I've seen, but I figured it out last night in my room.

"Just 'cause you see something on TV doesn't mean it's real," Garrett sneered. "You want to know what's real? This is."

He pressed the barrel so hard against Annie's head that she let out a tiny squeak.

"Annie, don't worry. He's not going to shoot you."

"Don't be so sure."

"Oh, I'm certain of it. And I'll tell you why in a minute. But first, I want to go back to what you just said about what's real and not. Let's start with the evidence in this case. The fact is there were only three people who had access to the hayloft that evening. You, the marshal, and Dallas Joshua James. We know what happened to James, so that rules him out as the killer— just like in the TV show. The marshal might have benefited from Bell's death, except he's not that stupid. The loan Bell made to Buckleberry would have tipped off the authorities and made the marshal the prime suspect. That leaves you."

"You're forgetting the old security guard."

"No, he didn't fit the TV plot. But more than that, the fact that you hinted he might have a reason to kill Bell proved he didn't do it. What I don't understand is why you didn't just kill Bell up here and toss his body into the gulch."

"And what? Have folks say the last time they saw Bill Bell alive was when he was riding up to Rattlesnake Gulch to see Deputy Garrett? No, folks needed to see Bill leave for the airport."

"How did you lure him into the barn?"

"Boy, I swear. If you don't stop moving toward that knife, I'm going to put a bullet in her shoulder socket. Be a mighty painful way to bleed out."

Annie began to sob. I gave up all hope of reaching the knife.

"I faked a call from that movie producer's assistant to get Bill to think he'd landed that part," Garrett said confidently. "Bill bragged to a few people at the canteen that he was heading to Hollywood. I asked him to meet me in Lazy Jack's. Told him there was a problem with one of the projectors, and I needed him to take a look before he left for the big lights. Bill always thought and acted like he knew more about the theatrical equipment than the rest of us. I played to his ego and it worked. The idea was to pop him and dump his body later in a place where the critters would find it."

"But then James arrived," I offered.

"Pulled right into that barn in his sporty Dodge Charger like he owned the place. Surprised he didn't hear the gunshot. Might have too, if that car of his wasn't so blasted loud. I hid behind the bales of hay, watching. He looked around for Earp's gun and didn't find it. 'Course, that's 'cause I had it. Instead of driving to the employee lot, he just left the car in the barn with the keys in the ignition. He did that a lot. Later he'd pay one of the hands a few bucks to park it for him. Gave me the perfect place to dump the body."

"So you knew about James phoning Mr. Earp and asking to borrow his Schofield?"

"Of course I knew. That wasn't the first time James had needed to borrow the gun. That old codger always hung it on the same peg in the first stall. I figured if someone *did* find the revolver they would pin the murder on either Earp or James but not me."

"But I showed up."

"Bad timing for me, but it's all going to work out."

"I know you used an IP-spoofing program to route the calls to a phone-tree program and dial the marshal at set times to make it appear that Bill Bell was in Los Angeles, but how did you clone Bell's voice?"

"One of the things a mall cop has is lots of time on his hands. I got pretty good at chatting up the tech guys at the wireless store. They showed me some neat ways to hack into a person's voice mail and download their calls. Strung together a few audio files with Bill's words from his voice mail greeting. Not too hard if you know what you're doing—which I did."

I broke eye contact with Garrett and gave Annie a sympathetic look. "Sorry I had to trick you into helping me, but I couldn't think of any other way to make sure he'd follow you up here."

Her face twisted with confusion. "What ... do you mean, tricked me?"

"In the blacksmith shop. I knew you'd probably check with the coroner to see if what I said was true about James being hit on the head. Once the coroner confirmed it," I said to Annie, "your only chance of staying alive was to find your uncle and tell him everything, including how you'd seen Deputy Garrett in the graveyard that night and how someone, probably the deputy, clubbed you on the head as a warning to keep quiet."

"I *did* talk to my uncle before I went to the mine. How'd you …"

Her look of bewilderment was replaced by anger. "You tricked me!"

"Sorry, but I didn't have a choice. I needed him to confess." I moved my hand to my jacket pocket. "Don't shoot," I told Garrett. "I want to get this digital recorder out to check and make sure it recorded everything."

I hit the rewind button and played a short segment. The quality of the recording was excellent.

I took a tentative step toward Annie.

"Stop right there."

"It's over, Deputy." Keeping my eyes on the gun, I moved closer.

"I'm warning you, boy."

"Question is, which of us do you shoot first? Annie or me?" Another step. "Try for me and she'll go for the knife. Might get it, too. And if she's as good with a blade as she is with Mr. Earp's Schofield …"

I took another step.

Garrett swung the gun away from Annie's head and fired at me. I couldn't help but jump. But I didn't fall back, nor did I clutch my chest as the farmer had. Instead I simply shook my head while trying to clear the ringing in my ears. A puzzled look contorted Garrett's face. He must've been wondering how he could have missed at such a close range when the door behind me burst open and Wyatt Earp entered.

Aiming his shotgun at Garrett, Mr. Earp tossed me a pair of plastic handcuffs and said, "Deputy Caden, would you mind doing the honors?"

Garrett, still eyeing the smoking gun in disbelief, made no attempt to resist.

"Deputy Garrett, you of all people should know to inspect your weapon before heading out into the field," I said, picking up the gun. "Especially in a ghost town that uses blanks for bullets."

I handed the Glock to Earp. "I believe this is how the ghost gunfights work, is it not?"

Earp smiled. I took Annie by the arm and helped her up. "Thanks for wanting to keep an eye on me," I said, thumbing back a strand of her hair.

"Now let's go get Billy the Kid's body out of that car."

CHAPTER TWENTY-ONE
ONE HERO FOR A DAY

Marshal Buckleberry found Billy the Kid's body in the trunk of the Charger. Pat Garrett was charged with two counts of first-degree murder, one count of killing a bear, one count of attempted murder (*me*), kidnapping, and assault with a deadly weapon. Other charges remained pending. For the remainder of the week, I was the hero of Deadwood. No need to call the media. As soon as the sheriff radioed that Bill Bell's body had been found, the journalists wheeled around and raced back. Had Buckleberry spent a hundred grand with a media firm, he could not have received better advertising.

BILLY THE KID AND JESSE JAMES GUNNED DOWN IN DEADWOOD. COUNTY MEDICAL

EXAMINER CALLS KILLING, "WORSE THAN THE
SHOOTOUT AT O.K. CORRAL."

The *Santa Rosa Gazette* featured my picture on the front
page. The local NBC affiliate ran my interview on the home
page of their website. The editor of *Cool Ghoul Magazine* called
the marshal and asked if he could interview the "ghost detective." I told the marshal I'd have to think about it—that I
might be busy with another murder case for a while.

"What case?" Mom asked. We stood on the bottom of the
bunkhouse steps passing Dad our luggage.

"Yeah, Nick. What case?" my sister repeated.

Annie arrived carrying a straw basket full of fruit, flowers,
and vintage books. She presented the basket to my sister, adding, "Something to remember us by."

Wendy squealed with delight. "This is awesome! *Dust and
Diamond*. I so love Donn Taylor's poetry. Thanks, Annie."

"What about me?" I said. "Don't I get something as a
keepsake?"

Annie peered into my eyes, her face softening. "Well ... I
was hoping to surprise you in the hayloft later. But since you
asked."

She pulled my face close to hers and, pressing her cheek
against mine, whispered, "I've been keeping a secret. My uncle
never told me to keep an eye on you."

"Oh? Is that the gift?"

She cupped my head in her hands, turned my face close
to hers, and pulled me down, kissing me on the forehead like
a small child. I couldn't understand why until my eyes found
the silver cross resting against her soft skin. She released me,
unhooked the clasp, and placed the necklace around my neck.

"Not for good luck," she said quietly, "but for a good life."

She kissed me quickly on the lips and hurried off.

"Wow. That was awkward," my sister remarked. "Maybe you two should get a room."

"Wendy!"

"Sorry, Mom. Just saying …"

"Speaking of just saying," Mom said curtly, "what's this other case you *think* you're investigating, son?"

"We better hit the road," I responded. "We have a long drive ahead of us."

"It's not *that* long, son."

"It might be if we have to go by way of Dallas."

"Dallas! What's in Dallas?"

"I phoned a professor at a divinity school down there. Said I was investigating the disappearance of a man named Jesus Christ, and I understood the body went missing and was never found. He said if I stopped by he'd be more than happy to go over the circumstances surrounding the man's death with me."

"Mom," Wendy bleated. "Make him stop. Please?"

"Lots to see on the drive down," Wyatt Earp piped up. "Got a haunted mansion in Denver, writers' college in Colorado Springs, and a Cadillac ranch in Amarillo."

"Cadillac ranch? Then it's settled," said Dad. "Dallas it is."

"Frank!"

"You know how I've always wanted a Caddy, hon." Gesturing toward our waiting toaster car, Dad added, "saddle up and let's ride."

LEGEND OF THE DEAD MAN'S HAND

The dead man's hand is a two-pair poker hand, namely "aces and eights." This card combination gets its name from a legend that it was the hand held by Wild Bill Hickok when he was murdered on August 2, 1876, in Saloon No. 10 at Deadwood, South Dakota.

The real town of Deadwood, South Dakota, is named for the dead trees found in its gulch. Deadwood was famous during the "wild west" for its lawless reputation, gunfights, and killings. Deadwood gained fame for the murder of Wild Bill Hickok, gunslinger and lawman. Jack McCall was found guilty of Hickok's murder and hanged.

FOR FURTHER INVESTIGATION

Questions written by Sarah Lynn Phillips

1. Ghosts! Early in the book Nick said there was no such thing as a ghost. But as time went on, he wasn't so sure. What do you think? What evidence supports your answer?

2. Nick made the following statement: "Just because you believe in vampires, werewolves, and witches, doesn't mean they're real." What do you think? How do you determine what's real and what isn't?

3. Nick found a Bible that had stories of ghosts and other odd happenings highlighted in yellow. Take a closer look at these passages.

- 1 Samuel 28:3-20 – A Midnight Meeting with a Dead Man

- Matthew 14:22-33 – A Ghost Walking on Water?

- Matthew 27:50-53 – Earthquake, Open Graves, Walking Dead

4. What would you say if someone told you they saw a ghost?

5. Jesus died, but three days later his tomb was found open and empty of all but the grave clothes (Luke 24:1-12). Do a little detective work with Nick. Investigate where he was seen. By whom? For how long?

- Luke 24:13-16, 28-32, 36-43, 50-53

- John 20:11-30; 21:1, 4-14

- Acts 1:3

6. Using the evidence found in Question 5, what clues can you find that show how Jesus appeared to be different after he died? How do these descriptions of a "dead Jesus" differ from how movies and books normally portray ghosts?

7. Nick tells Mr. Earp, "My sister is sure she's seen a ghost. She says when we die that's it. No heaven or hell. We only end up wandering earth looking for our bodies." Spy out other opinions about what happens when people die.

- Jesus: John 14:1-3; Luke 23:39-43

- Paul: 2 Corinthians 5:6-8; Philippians 1:23, 24

8. Wyatt Earp never thought about heaven until his wife got sick. What causes people to think about life after death?

9. Do the decisions we make now have consequences after we die? Check out the vision of John in Revelation 20:12.

10. In Chapter 18, Mr. Earp told Nick, "Those lies we believe about our lives are the real ghosts that haunt us . . . . Those whispering voices that tear us down and leave us feeling worthless and ugly. It's those spooks you need to be worried about." What are some secret "what-ifs, wish I hadn't, and I'm not good enough" statements that bother you?

CADEN CHRONICLES
SKULL CREEK STAKEOUT

BOOK TWO

CHAPTER ONE
A CASE I CAN SINK MY TEETH INTO

Death found me on a hot June morning in Walt Disney World's Tower of Terror.

Minutes before I heard about the vampire in Transylvania, North Carolina, I pulled the seat belt across my waist and showed my hands to the bellhop. Behind me buckles snapped shut; arms shot up. The smiling service attendant in his maroon and gold cap bid us a pleasant stay at the Hollywood Hotel and retreated into the boiler room. Service doors sealed us inside, and the elevator yanked us up.

The young boy seated next to me whispered to his mom, "Why did he make us raise our hands?"

"So when they snap our picture it looks like we're having fun."

"And to prove you're not holding anything in your hand," I offered. "See, if you place a penny on your palm, like this, when the car drops the coin will—"

"Don't you dare try that, Grayson!" said the boy's mom, glaring at me.

I shoved the penny back in my pocket and muttered, "Wasn't suggesting he do it. Just saying that's why they make you put your hands up."

The car stopped on the thirteenth floor. Doors opened. Our elevator car rumbled down a darkened hallway, and the theme song from the *Twilight Zone* began playing through headrest speakers. A short ways in front, Rod Serling magically appeared, warning riders: "You unlock this door with the key of imagination. Beyond it is another dimension—a dimension of sound, a dimension of sight, a dimension of mind. You're moving into a land of both shadow and substance, of things and ideas. You've just crossed over into... *(dramatic pause)...* the Twilight Zone."

Instantly a barrage of objects shot past—a wooden door, Einstein's formula for relativity, an eyeball. Windowpanes shattered and shards of glass morphed into twinkling stars. Through the speakers a little girl began singing, "It's raining, it's pouring..."

Buried in my front pocket my smart phone began vibrating. I pulled it out and quickly read the text message. "PHONE

ME NOW. RIGHT NOW! GOT KILLER OF A STORY
FOR YOU! – Calvin."

Right, I thought. *Bet it's just another zombie fest or supposed
house haunting.*

See, weeks earlier I'd signed on to be a reporter for the
Cool Ghoul Gazette—an online website dedicated to exploring
ghosts, zombies, werewolves, vampires and all things super-
natural and freaky. We have a huge readership in the Briton.
Ghosts sightings are huge over there. Anyway, for months my
parents had been after me to get a summer job. Mom thought
I needed to start saving for college. Dad kept saying it was time
I did something other than sit around and watch TV, even
though watching TV *is* my job.

No kidding. Watching television (online, mostly) is my job.
I'm a founding member of TV Crime Watchers, a group of
teens that analyzes and catalogues crime, cop, and detective
shows. We have a huge database of episodes going back almost
thirty years, and we use this information to catch real murderers. At least, when law enforcement officials will let us help.
Our little group has an eighty percent close rate. That means
in most cases we can correctly identify the killer *before* the real
detectives can. Problem is, TV Crime Watchers doesn't pay,
and making money is apparently a big deal. Especially for my
mom and dad. Our family is a victim of what Dad calls, "the
Great Recession."

I think what he means is that we're middle class poor.

Before our trip to Disney, he was complaining about how
his pension at the automotive parts company was wiped out
in the stock market. Mom thinks we should sell our home,

but according to the real estate company Mom works for, our house is worth less now than when we bought it. The only way we could afford the trip to Disney was to drive two days in our ten-year-old Buick and stay in a three-star motel on the outskirts of Orlando. So yeah, right now having a job is tops in our family.

"Can't pay for the good life without a good job," Dad keeps reminding me. "And sometimes, you can't even pay for it, then."

Dad hoped I'd get a job cutting grass like my cousin Fred. Fred has like a gazillion customers. He made enough last summer to buy his own truck—a used Ford Ranger that has over a hundred thousand miles on it and leaks oil like a Gulf oil well.

But I'm not Fred.

To me the idea of working outside all summer and coming home sweaty and tired is, well… work. Mom was after me to get a job dog sitting, but the last thing I wanted to do was to spend my summer picking up poop in a plastic bag. That's just gross.

So after our trip to Deadwood Canyon, when I solved the murder of one of the ghost town's actors, I landed the job at the *Cool Ghoul Gazette,* and now my editor was texting me with a "killer" assizgnment that I was pretty sure would be a huge waste of my time because most of the stuff he sends me is.

The elevator car stopped. Another set of doors opened, this time revealing a bird's eye view of Walt Disney World's Hollywood Studios theme park. Crowds choked Sunset Boulevard and moved in random directions like energetic ants bent on beating the other ants to the top the hill. Children lined up near a pretzel stand to get Buzz Lightyear's autograph. Parents milled about in the designated stroller area.

Our car dropped.

Girls screamed. Kids shrieked. Not me. You couldn't have blasted the smile off my face with a power washer. Down we plummeted! Sudden stop, then rocket back up. Once more doors peeled open, and the park flashed before us. Again we fell. Up and down we went with cables yanking us both directions. I'd learned about the cables from watching the Discovery Channel. It seems the initial design of the Tower proved too tame. The head of the design team complained that if his tie didn't fly up and hit him in the face the car wasn't falling fast enough. So they added cables underneath the car, and now when you fall the cable jerks you down at a rate of almost two Gs. It's way better than just jumping off a building.

Our car fell the final time and stopped. Doors opened. Buckles unsnapped. Passengers rushed across the lobby of the old hotel toward the photo counter to see themselves on video monitors.

I checked the floorboard for my phone.

"I think you're looking for this," said Grayson's mom, thrusting my phone at me. "It nearly hit me in the face."

"I'm sorry. I meant to—"

"There's no place for that on a ride with kids. Someone could get hurt."

"I know," I said. "I'm very sorry."

"Children are very impressionable at this age, and when they see an older boy doing something like this…"

"Look, I said I'm sorry. I didn't mean to have it out. It's just that my editor texted me, and I was looking at the screen when…"

But Grayson's mom, having loudly made her point in front of the other riders, turned away and marched toward the monitors, pulling Grayson along.

I hung back, waited for the crowd to thin and aimed my phone at the monitor and snapped a picture of the picture of myself. Outside I found Mom and Dad and Wendy waiting for me at the Fast Past gate.

Dad said, "Well? How was it?"

"Awesome! Can I go again?"

"Maybe after lunch," Mom said. "If we have time. We're supposed to be at the ESPN Sports Complex by four."

"She has to be there," I said, cutting my eyes toward Wendy. "Not me."

"We're *all* going," Mom countered. "Your sister's cheerleading is a big deal, and we're going to be there for her."

"Yeah?" said, Wendy, mounting her virtual high horse. "For once we're doing something *I* want to do."

What do you mean "for once," I wanted to scream. *That's all we ever do.*

Talk It Up!

Want free books?
First looks at the best new fiction?
Awesome exclusive merchandise?

We want to hear from you!

Give us your opinions on titles, covers, and stories.
Join the Z Street Team.

Email us at zstreetteam@zondervan.com
to sign up today!

Also—Friend us on Facebook!

www.facebook.com/goodteenreads

- Video Trailers
- Connect with your favorite authors
- Sneak peeks at new releases
- Giveaways
- Fun discussions
- And much more!